I0557807

LOVERS
OF
OLD
FILMS

Ophelia Finsen

Copyright © Louise Clark 2008
All rights reserved. No part of this book may be used or reproduced in any
manner whatsoever without the written permission of the copyright owner.
Cover art and design copyright © Louise Clark 2008

Published using Lulu.com
ISBN 978-0-9559923-0-8

PART ONE

His mother dropped the cup as she was wiping the dust off with a damp cloth. It hit the kitchen floor and broke into two neat pieces.

"Oh goodness." She sounded startled, as if aware of the cup for the first time.

Edward glanced away from the open cupboard. "It doesn't matter."

She bent down and picked up the cup. "But now you only have five teacups."

"It doesn't matter," he repeated. "It's only me living here. I'll just have to wash up more often."

"Now, Edward," she smiled at him, as if she was humouring a simple-minded child. As if he were still five. He would be twenty-three soon. He was a man. Just out of the student uniform, but still a long way from the middle-aged cares of full sets of matching teacups.

"What's this?" Edward's father entered the kitchen, carrying a large box of pots and pans from the car. "You getting distracted there, Jean?"

"Just that woman who suddenly ran out across the road."

They all stepped up to the kitchen window, and stared out from the first floor to the passing road outside. Cars droned by. Virtually opposite the building there was a bus stop. A woman was waiting, curiously dressed for the middle of the day. It looked as if she were going to a cocktail party.

"That woman?" Edward asked, pointing.

"Don't point." His mother slapped his hand. She didn't remind him that it was rude to stare on this occasion though. "It's been years since I saw anyone with a fur stole. Do you suppose it's real fur?"

"That glamour puss," his father commented. "I passed her on the stairs."

One of his neighbours. Edward peered a little closer. Everything about the woman suggested a lightness of bounce. Clothed in white: a dress and a shawl made to look like the pelt of a dead animal (if not the real thing); she oozed honey-sun warmth from her Mediterranean skin. She was his neighbour? She looked far too glamorous for this dreary English day.

"Maybe she's going to a fancy dress party," his mother said, turning away from the window.

"Maybe," Edward murmured, forgetting himself. The woman abruptly shifted her gaze to stare up at the building. Straight into his eye. Edward jumped back from the window, embarrassed. The woman flashed a smile in his direction, then lent out to wave at the approaching bus.

His mother touched his arm. "Shall we go down and help your father get the last of the cases out of the car?"

"Sure." He looked out the window again, but the bus was driving away and the woman was gone.

Two days later saw the demise of Edward's excitement for his new home. He had been in residence for three days, and never bumped into any of his neighbours. He hadn't seen anyone. Surely these people had to go out: work, food, fresh air, anything. If only to leave the flat to remind themselves this wasn't just a dream.

It was a small block of flats, four floors with two flats per floor and the single stairwell. No lift. An average looking building, it was nestled in the northern suburbs that sprawled out from York. Far enough away from the centre so that the rent was affordable if you wanted to live on your own.

He was disappointed. This was the first time he'd lived alone, but not his first experience of living in flats. As a student, living in makeshift furnished rooms, keeping odd hours and a fantastic social life, he had always been bumping into neighbours. The permanently stoned Irish lads downstairs, the hard-drinking girls to the left, the shy awkward students with virginal eyes downcast, even the out-of-touch academic types had made an attempt. Here everyone was hidden, isolated. This 'grown-up life' was very disappointing.

Entering the building, he paused at the foot of the stairs, examining the two ground floor residences for signs of life. There was nothing on one of the doors; on the other someone had rather childishly stuck a brightly coloured sign saying 'Lexie' above the spyhole. It made it look like the doorway to a five-year-old's bedroom. It was something at least.

Edward moved towards the door, not certain whether he would have dared to knock, or just try and spy from the wrong end of the hole. Footsteps hurrying down the stairwell suddenly frightened him. His heart pounding as if they'd caught a peeping tom.

There was laughter; a suave female voice accompanied by a real manly chortle. Edward looked up expectedly. The couple came down the staircase, side by side and blocking oncoming traffic. The man, built like a rugby player with a look of intellectual arrogance, had stopped laughing, but the woman was still amused, her bright red lips stretched across perfect teeth. She was glossy, smoothed to perfection. Long, waved hair that never seemed to shift in position.

Neither of them saw Edward.

"Now, Margaret," the man drawled.

"Margaret?" The woman slapped playfully at his arm. "What's come over you now?"

For a moment he felt alive in human company again, then they were out the door and he was alone. Working wasn't quite what he had expected, although it had only been two days, he told himself as he started up the staircase. He hadn't been invited in to any of the little cliques at the office. No one invited him back to the pub after work. No one seemed to notice him. But it was only his first week. Everyone said the first week was hellish. Then it all fell into place.

One flight of stairs and he was home. He glanced up the continuing steps, wondering who was up there. Didn't really matter, one way or another. Edward put his key in the lock, then stopped. It felt as though someone was watching him.

The door opposite to his own was blank. There was a slot next to the doorbell where someone's name had been written, but this had been aggressively scribbled out. The door seemed to shrink back under his attention. Cautiously, he stepped across the landing and put his eye to the spyhole. He couldn't see anything looking through the wrong way, but he felt someone lurch back. Someone scared.

His mobile started ringing.

"Shit!" he cursed, embarrassed that it had made him jump. "Yeah, Toby?" he answered, turning on his heel back to the flat. "How's the job going?"

"Shite," Toby grumbled. "Another day on the fucking photocopier. I spent enough time on that at uni…"

Edward shuddered, remembering the drunken night Toby had stripped off and run around campus before getting into the photocopying room. The print offs had given the librarians something to think about the next day.

"After all those years studying, you'd think they'd realise I'm capable of a bit more than photocopying. I said that to my boss today."

"Yeah?"

"Yeah."

"The dwarf cow?"

"That's the one. She gave me some crap about starting somewhere, learning the ropes."

"Right." Edward flopped into his great aunt's old settee. Toby thought of himself as a high-flying lawyer. He'd been lucky to land that job in such a well-thought of solicitors in the city centre, but the way he talked about it, you'd think no one else working there had ever been to university.

"You got any plans for Friday?"

The start of a long weekend alone. He'd moved to York because the potential of the graduate training scheme had sounded good and he remembered it as a pretty town from childhood outings. He didn't know anyone in York, and he'd been lucky that one of his friends from university, Toby, had got a job there too. Lucky coincidence. Toby had moved into a flat share of young professionals, but Edward had found a reasonably priced flat on the outskirts of the town and decided he would try the proper grown-up life of living alone.

"We need to get smashed."

Toby's words interrupted his melancholia.

"On Friday?"

"Of course on bloody Friday. I don't intend being in any state for getting up the next day."

"All right, where do you want to meet? Know any good pubs?"

Toby snorted. "I don't know this bloody place. We'll just meet somewhere in town. A landmark."

They lived in different parts of town: Toby towards the south, Edward to the far north. It wasn't practical for one of them to travel to the other's flat.

"How about the Minster? That's pretty big."

Toby laughed crassly. "Yeah, you bloody bible basher. I'll see you there. Six sharpish."

"Arsewipe."

"See you."

On Wednesday there was a trail of plastic supermarket bags cluttering the entrance. A well-rounded girl, under twenty-five (you could tell from the jeans that were too tight for her hips, making her pasty flesh look like it had been squeezed out of the top of a tube under extreme pressure). Her ironed-straight long blonde hair swung like a pendulum as she wrestled with a key and her door. The door called Lexie.

"Ah, come on with you," she cajoled the door. She was struggling because as well as trying to unlock the door she was holding a bowling ball carrier styled handbag and trying to text on a mobile phone laden with dangling trinkets.

She swung her dumpy mass around when she heard Edward step over her shopping. "Hiya," she burst out. "You're not the new one are you?" she asked, her accent distinctly Glaswegian.

Edward took in the over-plucked eyebrows, the chubby cheeks and the glittery T-shirt and thought to himself, this girl is still in her teens. "I moved in at the weekend," he said, feeling a little awkward by her brashness.

"E. Gable," she said loudly, tossing her mobile phone into a bag of shopping. "It's on your label by the doorbell," she added by way of explaining how she knew. "I'm Lexie."

"Yeah, I saw." He pointed at the door.

She turned around to look at the door as if she didn't know there was anything there. "Oh yeah, that wee thing," she giggled. "I put it there for a bit of a laugh. It's a really nice place here; everyone's so nice. It's got a real family feel."

He looked at her incredulously. She couldn't mean this block of flats, could she? Someone as bubbly as she was couldn't possibly mistake this graveyard for friendly. "You mean York?"

"York?" Her eyebrow lines shot up. "Oh yeah, I suppose, it's like a wee village in a way. But I meant here, the block. They're a great bunch. You've met them, right?"

"You're the first person that's spoken to me."

"What? No way. So you haven't even had the welcoming committee?" She tapped her chin with a glittery fingernail. "I'll have to get on to him about that. You coming in for a cuppa?"

"Oh, I'd better..." he made a move for the stairwell.

"Carry some bags in, make yourself useful."

Lexie disappeared into her flat, leaving Edward outside with all of the shopping. "I..." he started to make excuses, but it seemed pointless when there was no one to listen. He ought not to complain, he thought as he picked up her shopping, noting the number of crisps and biscuits. Someone here was actually trying to make contact. That had to be promising. Even if she was a mad Glaswegian teenager.

"I'm from Glasgow," she told him as she put the kettle on.

"I'd noticed," Edward told her as he looked around her flat. It seemed a lot smaller than his.

"The accent's kind of telling, right?" Lexie watched him. "My flat's a wee tight arsehole of a place, I know. The communal bike lock up takes some of my floor space. Mind you, I'm not complaining. The rent's really low, and I couldn't afford anything more. I work at the supermarket on Haxby highstreet. You know it?"

Edward shook his head. "I've only been living here three days."

"Of course you have," Lexie said, laughing and slapping him on the back. "What do you do with yourself?"

"I'm on a graduate training scheme with Atlas Insurance." He winced as the words were out of his mouth. They sounded so pompous outside of university.

"Ooo, an intellectual," Lexie twisted a tress of hair around her finger, impressed that he had such a job. "Well, you're going to enjoy living here. Just wait till you've met everyone. We're going to have great fun."

Edward looked at the way she was staring at him and worried what exactly she meant by that.

The welcoming committee, as Lexie had put it, arrived later that evening. She'd worked fast after he'd finished his tea. At least he could only presume they were the one and the same, because when he opened the door the first thing the man said was: "I'm the welcoming committee."

Edward had been slopped out across the settee watching mindless television when there had been a confident, sharp and energetic knock at the door. He crept up to the door, hoping it wasn't Lexie. Peering through the spy hole, he saw a dark haired man of indeterminate age. His golden tan looked very out of place for this time of the year, as did the formal suit.

He looked vaguely familiar but Edward couldn't place where he had seen him before. But his overall appearance radiated guarantees that he could be explicitly trusted.

Edward opened the door.

"I'm the welcoming committee," the man burst out, friendly, his arms open in welcome. "Edward, isn't it?"

"Yeah," Edward mumbled, feeling distinctly inferior in his soup-splattered T-shirt and jogging bottoms. The man was dressed in what looked like a very, very expensive suit.

"Archie." The man offered his hand, grabbing Edward's in a warm and hearty shake. "I live up on the top floor. I'm sorry we've left you for a couple of days. I've been down in London on business. I'm sure you'll get acquainted with the others soon enough. In the meantime, we hope you'll be very happy here. And this is for you."

He offered a bottle of rust-coloured liquid. Edward accepted, taken aback by the generosity. He felt guilty for having cursed the mediocrity of adult-life, for longing back to his student days. This was definitely an improvement.

"I don't know what to say," he started, a little overwhelmed.

Archie flashed him a smile. "That's a good bottle of bourbon. The furnishing of every flat has got to start somewhere. Please don't think me rude, but I'm on my way to a charity ball, so I can't stop and help you crack it open."

"We'll save it for another night."

"Sure will." Another smile and he was nimbly strutting down the staircase.

Edward looked down at the bottle. Things were certainly looking up.

He was leaving the flat to take a walk to the corner shop when he saw her for the first time. He'd just locked his door, when he heard the downstair's main entrance slam shut. Delicate, but hurried footsteps moved up to the first floor. A willowy girl with long, loose brown hair appeared, her body shrouded in a sheepskin jacket. She clutched textbooks and a ringbinder to her chest. Her eyes were downcast, studiously at the floor. Edward got the impression that if he hadn't been there she would have been more comfortable. She took a bunch of keys out of her pocket and went to silent little door opposite his.

"Excuse me," Edward boldly stepped forward. He wouldn't have usually bothered such obviously introverted neighbours, but after Lexie and Archie's welcomes, this girl didn't seem to quite fit.

She jumped, startled, and looked around at him, her big round eyes staring. She looked like a deer caught in headlights. She was entrancingly beautiful.

"I'm Edward," he began, stepping forward. "I just moved in…"

She clutched her books even tighter. Saying nothing.

He pointed at his door. "We're neighbours."

Her lips parted as if she would speak.

"Edward, is that your feet I see at the top of the stairs?" Lexie's voice charged brashly up ahead of her.

Edward glanced irritatedly down the stairs as Lexie appeared into view. "Yeah."

There was a slam and when he looked back, the girl had gone and the silent door was back in place.

"I've been having a great idea," Lexie continued as she trundled up towards him. "We should all try to get together, get to meet us all. I could do with a night out. We should have a building outing this Friday. Tomorrow, right?"

"Oh, I'm meeting up with a mate on Friday."

"That's great. The more the merrier. We'll have a great laugh. You'll meet the crowd. Have you met the welcoming committee yet?"

"Archie?"

She broke out into a warm smile. "Archie. He's so nice."

"Yeah. He gave me a bottle of bourbon. Can you believe it? Bourbon of all things?"

"Really?" She looked surprised. "He told me that it was the standard welcome gift, but he wouldn't give me one because he said young ladies like me shouldn't drink hard spirits. This is me we're talking about; I've been drinking since I was thirteen. Anyways, I was eighteen when I moved in here. It wasn't illegal or anything."

Eighteen? She was older than he'd guessed.

"Turned nineteen a few months later as well," she continued, more to herself than for his information. "But he gave you bourbon. You don't look much older than me."

"I'm twenty-three soon," he said defensively, suddenly feeling the need to push his age as far away from hers as possible. He should have told her he'd be thirty in seven years' time.

"Ah, I should have known," she waggled a finger at him. "You've been to university, you're an old man now."

He wasn't sure if she was mocking him.

"I never even finished my Highers," she added wistfully. "Anyways, Friday night we'll all go out together. Show you the town. It'll be fun. I'm a real party animal."

He didn't doubt it.

Toby hadn't been overly impressed when Edward explained how the other people in his building wanted to come as well. Toby had picked up when he had been assured that there would be women. Edward was a little slower to get in the spirit, but by the time Lexie called to remind him, he had actually said he was looking forward to the outing.

Lexie was growing on Edward. She wasn't perfect: larger than life, still with elements of the annoying teenager; but she was good fun, chatty, and far better than sitting on his own on a Friday evening wondering if this was all there was. She could cheer anyone up, with her funny, down-to-earth, if simplistic way of looking at things.

He'd gone home after work and got ready before going downstairs to Lexie's. She was more giddy than usual – she'd been drinking. Getting ready for the night out. She gave him a shot of vodka whilst she scrabbled round in her bedroom looking for high heels.

They got the bus into town, meeting Toby outside York Minster. He looked grumpy, awkwardly loitering. His eyes widened when he saw Lexie, who playfully slapped him on the back with her small beaded handbag, before tottering off in front of them bawling, "Come on boys!"

Toby turned to Edward. "She'd a bit big."

"She's a good laugh."

Toby grinned wickedly. "I don't mind them with a bit of meat on them."

"We're meeting Sophia at the Bar Jax," Lexie shouted over her shoulder as they headed down Coney Street.

Toby's eyes lit up even more, although still determinedly focused on Lexie's wobbling backside. "And who is Sophia?"

"She lives at the flats." Lexie stopped to look back at them. "And she's way out of your league," she added, more for Toby's benefit. She didn't even look at Edward. As if no one would even consider him a potential seducer. He felt a little offended. No one noticed. "I tried to get Ray to come out with us, but he wouldn't," she continued, wedging herself between them and slipping an arm through each respective on either side. "He never does. He likes to drink and smoke at home alone. Funny old bugger. Ray." She glanced at Edward. "He lives in the flat below yours."

"Oh right."

"And Margaret lives above you."

"What about the girl opposite me?" Thinking of the three-dimensional layout of the building, he was back on the landing, staring into the deep dark pools that were that silent girl's eyes. "What's she called?"

"Oh, is this the bar?" Toby interrupted. Lexie clapped her hands and clattered across the road and Edward's question was forgotten, if it had ever been noticed to begin with.

Inside, it was the kind of atmospherically-lit, sensual place that you'd expect to be dimmed with the haze of cigarette smoke, except that the smoking ban meant that your vision was clear and your nasal palette full of other people's sweat and cheap perfume. Edward didn't smoke, so he wasn't bothered, and stale cigarettes was one of the worst smells known to man and yet there was something still almost sophisticated about the wisps of smoke twirling off the end of a lit cigarette. Despite the health risks, the cost and the long-term detrimental effect on beauty, there was still something alluring about it all. The enclosed private intensity of lighting up. The adult look of exhaling smoke.

The music in Bar Jax was loud, but not so loud that you couldn't speak. It was grown-up; nothing of the techno churned-out electronica of the student meat markets. Lexie led the way through the tables and people, looking for the illusive Sophia, whoever she was.

"Sophia, there you are!"

The two young men followed the girl to a table in one of the back corners. Sophia was sat alone, a definition of sophistication with a cocktail set in front of her at the table. She was dressed up in a sleeveless, square-necked dress; the kind of thing you saw in the windows of the more expensive boutiques. Her hair was loose – albeit carefully styled – but there was no mistaking her: it was definitely the woman they'd seen waiting at the bus stop the day he'd moved in.

"Is Archie not coming?" Lexie asked.

A flicker of a scowl crossed Sophia's face. Her brows knitted, her bottom lip stuck out in a mouth that on closer inspection was born to pout. The irritation was quickly smoothed over. "He had to take some business associates out." She watched as Lexie shuffled around the narrow space between chairs and table to drop herself beside Sophia. "Lexie, darling, couldn't you have worn a dress?" she asked, looking disapprovingly at Lexie's squeezed toothpaste jeans.

Lexie ignored her. "Sophia, this is Edward, he's just moved in. And this is Edward's friend, Toby."

Sophia flashed them a smile. "How wonderful to meet you." On certain points her accent sounded almost upper class, but it wasn't British. It was a curious affectation that had been learned unconsciously.

"Nice to meet you, Soph'." Toby pushed himself forward. "You're not English are you?"

Sophia raised her eyebrows in response.

His over-confidence faltered a little. Sophia was a young woman, but she looked like she was in her late twenties, and her maturity was starting to overpower him.

"Well, I mean, your English is fantastic, but you have an accent," he stammered.

"How kind of you to say so," she said, sounding slightly sarcastic. "I'm from Italy."

"Italy, I knew it," Toby clicked his fingers. "Italian women are the best."

Lexie had been right, Sophia was out of their league.

"When's Margaret coming?" Lexie asked loudly, breaking up the awkward silence but only making it worse.

"Why do you always call her Margaret?" Sophia asked back as if Lexie's question were unimportant.

Lexie shrugged. "She said I could."

Sophia settled back into her seat as if to say this explanation would have to do for the time being. "Lexie, why don't you and Toby go and get some drinks. Then I can get to know Edward a little better."

"Oh, all right then." Lexie sounded a little put out. Standing up, she made her way back around the table. Grabbing Toby by the arm, she grinned coyly at him. "Let's you and me go to the bar."

Toby grinned back. "Now you're talking my language."

Sophia patted the seat next to her. "Come and sit down, Edward. Tell me about yourself. I'm sorry the others couldn't come tonight, but you'll meet them all soon enough. Are you liking the flat?"

Edward set himself neatly on the seat next to her, feeling like a little boy. "It's a nice flat."

"It is. And there's such wonderful people living in the building. And what are you working with?"

"I've just started at Atlas Insurance."

"Oh really, and what do you do there?"

"I started on the graduate training programme."

"Oh, of course," she chirruped, reaching gracefully forward to pick up her cocktail glass.

"Start off on the photocopying and they'll give you something better to do in a few months."

He felt put in his place. "And what is it you do?"

"Can't you tell? I work in fashion." She lent away from him, pursing her duck lips and squinting her heavily made-up eyes as if trying to work out who he was. "What was your name again?"

"Edward…" She had a bad memory.

"No, no, no. I mean your full name."

"Edward Gable."

Sophia nodded as if this meant something. "I see."

Edward had drunk too much that Friday night. Even against the standard set by his student years, he'd really excelled. It had been good to think tomorrow didn't matter. That he could almost make it feel like the week hadn't happened. Getting used to a job was going to take longer than five days. In the meantime he had alcohol.

Sometime in the evening the rugby player he had seen in the stairwell had joined the gathering. It had turned out he wasn't a rugby player at all. He was a freelance arts correspondence or something equally impressive. Had a masterful voice, an intense stare and an aura around him making him impossible to be overlooked. Edward couldn't remember what he had said his name was. Had it been Orville or Oliver or something?

Sophia had left at half eleven. Oliver or whatever he was going by these days stayed to keep Edward company. Lexie and Toby had been all over each other. Not really aware of who the other was – both too intoxicated to think about what they did, or the fact that everyone in the bar could see. Passions hit a point and despite their inebriated state, they had conceded they had to change venue. Whisked away in a taxi; hardly the fairytale.

Oliver had laughed; it was probably the only thing to be done at such times. "You and me need a whisky after that performance," he had informed Edward. Stretching up to his imposing height, he had stridden over to the bar.

The alarm clock beeped at seven as if he were getting up for work. Edward cursed and pulled the plug. Thanking god he'd remembered to drink a pint of water before going to bed, he rolled over and disappeared back under the duvet.

The next time he woke up he'd just been dreaming about a pair of screeching falcons involved in air combat. There was a thud as something was dropped in the stairwell. Garbled shouting. Edward opened an eye. A door slammed with a force that ought to have brought down the supporting walls.

What the hell?

Staggering out of bed, Edward tramped to the door. He went to look through the spyhole, misjudged the distance and bumped his head on the door. There was nothing outside on the landing anyway.

He could definitely hear the muffled sound of shouting.

Edward opened his door as the facing door across the landing opened. The girl, loose hair and wearing a silk kimono, stepped forward to try and see the disturbance, noticed Edward and shrank back in the doorway. Edward took a couple of steps forward, no longer sure if he'd come out for the girl or the noise. There was a strangled silence.

"Cheap slut!"

That part of the argument was definitely audible. It was coming from downstairs. From Lexie's flat, but that particularly articulate insult hadn't been Lexie's voice.

A door opened somewhere upstairs.

"Archie!" Oliver's voice boomed. "Will you sort that mistress of yours out!"

Edward looked over at the girl. She opened her mouth to say something but no sound came out. She gestured back into her flat, coughed, then said: "Do you want to…?"

"Yes."

He followed her into her flat. The door was closed. The sound of the argument came through on another frequency here. Most of the words couldn't be made out, but the anger was more than apparent. Footsteps clattered down the stairwell outside. The girl put the kettle on. Edward looked down and realised he was wearing nothing but his boxers and that soup-stained T-shirt.

There was a pause in the shouting, and a third voice – this one deeper – joined the fray. It all blew up again. The girl took down cups from the cupboard. "Archie," she whispered. The argument spread out, blasting from different directions. Out on the stairwell. Footsteps clattered upwards. Lexie's flat became abruptly silent.

Edward shuffled awkwardly in the kitchen door. Hardly dressed for a visit to his neighbour. He didn't even know what he was doing here. "Thank god Oliver acted."

"Oliver?"

"Yeah, Oliver. He shouted for Archie."

"That's not his name," she told him. She dropped tea bags in the cups and poured in hot water. Never offered to update the gaps in Edward's knowledge.

He stood and watched her finish making the tea. Then followed her obediently into the living room. This flat was bigger than Lexie's but not as big as his own. The coffee table was piled with paper and open textbooks. The ringbinder he remembered her clutching. Tilting his head, he tried to read one of the pages in the open book. He couldn't understand it.

"You studying?" he asked as she passed him a cup of tea.

"Dutch."

"Oh. Right." He faltered. She sat down on the settee and just stared at him. "Are you a translator or something?" A translator? What a stupid question. She wouldn't have language textbooks like that if she was a translator. She'd be already fluent.

"No," she replied, not reacting as if it were a stupid question. "I work in records."

"Records?"

"At the hospital."

"Oh. Right."

"It's not very interesting." She smiled sadly and looked into her tea. "I've been there since I was eighteen. Nine years," she sighed wistfully and stared out of the window.

It was a lot of sentences all at once for someone who came across as terrified of people. Fearful of speaking, like admitting her own existence.

"I work in insurance," he told her.

She looked back around at him and smiled. The room lit up. "Well then, neither of us do anything very much interesting."

Edward met Toby in the Museum Gardens on his short lunch break. Mondays were never good. Toby looked rattled about something. His shirt was crinkled.

"Bloody pain in the arse day."

"Good start to the week then?"

"Yeah," Toby took a sip from the large cardboard coffee cup he had. "Did you see Lexie at all over the weekend?"

"Lexie? Not exactly," he paused, smiling craftily at Toby. "Why, are you missing her already? You two were fair going at it on Friday."

"I vaguely remember we did when we got back to her flat."

"Oh, you started long before then, in the bar."

"Christ." Toby ran a hand through his hair.

"Never mind. It gave Oliver something to laugh at. Although I don't think he's actually called Oliver."

"Oliver? I don't remember any Oliver."

"You were preoccupied."

"Lexie called me Saturday afternoon," Toby started to confide, not particularly bothered about a man who wasn't called Oliver whom he couldn't recall. "She was well weird. I suppose that was her being sober. She was asking me if I thought she was a cheap slut."

Cheap slut. The only words that they'd properly heard. "There was a big screaming match on Saturday afternoon. I live on the floor above and I heard it. In Lexie's flat. I think she was fighting with Sophia."

"Sophia?" Toby's face lit up with lust. "So Sophia and Lexie were fighting over me?"

"I never said that."

"Maybe that's where she got the cheap slut from. I told her she wasn't – everybody has one night stands now and then, right?"

Edward tried to remember the last night of any variety he'd had.

"It's nothing to crucify yourself over," Toby continued. "But I can kind of understand why Sophia might have called her that. Sophia is a woman with style."

"Ah, but you've got Lexie."

Toby snorted. "It was just a one night stand. I must have been drunk. I don't know what I was thinking. She's a nice enough girl, I suppose, but I need to do a lot better, do you know what I mean? Someone like me and someone like her."

"What's wrong with Lexie?"

"She's very young, very immature. Besides, a shop assistant and a solicitor: it hardly fits right, does it? Now someone like Sophia…"

"Is very out of your league," Edward finished for him. "I bet she's too old for you as well. She'll be in her thirties."

"So? Maybe she's looking for a young man to groom."

"I doubt it." Toby's arrogance never failed to surprise him. "Lexie's more your type. Closer to your age."

"Lexie," Toby sneered. "I'm not starting anything with her. Now there's a burden I can do without. She could do with loosing some weight as well, you know?"

Edward made no comment and watched a squirrel run up a tree.

That evening, as if their discussions had been broadcast across town, Lexie turned up at Edward's door with two plastic carrier bags full of crisps and brightly coloured packets of biscuits. Edward saw it and immediately presumed comfort eating. Toby must have been as blunt to her on the phone as he had been at lunch time.

"Hiya," she muttered, distinctly more downcast than usual. "I brought these over for you," she explained, dumping the bags in his kitchen.

For him? Edward had a quick poke through the bags before looking up at her. "Are these from your work? I didn't ask you to buy all this for me, did I? How much do I owe you?"

Lexie shook her head. "I'm having a clearout. If you don't want them, just give them to your mates or throw them out. I can't resist if they're in the cupboard so I'm emptying the flat. I could do with loosing a bit of weight, so I'm going on a diet."

"Is this Toby's effect?"

"Toby?" For a moment she looked as though she didn't know who he was talking about. "Oh, Toby," she nodded, recalling the man. "No, he has nothing to do with it. I need to go out for a walk now. I'll catch you later."

"Yeah, sure. And thanks for the crisps." Edward watched her leave, and felt for a moment that something more than a diet was beginning.

When he came home from work on Thursday, there was a large antique wooden desk set outside the main doors. The woman he had seen walking down the stairs with Oliver was sitting territorially on top. Dressed smartly in a pencil skirt and jacket, her hair tied up, she looked like a stranded secretary, reclining ever so slightly as if she thought the desk was actually a piano and she a sultry jazz singer about to start an act.

Her face brightened as she saw him approach. She noticed his existence this time. "Hello there," she called out, sitting up pertly. "It's Edward, isn't it?"

He approached a little cautiously. It was slightly unsettling the way they all must have been discussing him since he moved in. As if he told one person something, they'd all know before the day was finished. "Yes, it is," he said, although she didn't need it confirming. "And you must be Margaret."

"Margaret!" she laughed. "Only my old Scottish mother calls me that. Well, her and Lexie. It must be a Scottish thing. But everyone else calls me Rita."

"Oh, right." Why did the women living here always manage to make him feel foolish? "Well, hello, Rita." Nothing more to say. He looked at his shoes, then to the piece of furniture she was still sitting on. "Nice desk you've got there."

"It is, isn't it?" She ran a hand down the length of the desk. He doubted she meant the action to be provocative, but she was the kind of woman who couldn't help but be that way all the time. "I work at home, so I thought I'd treat myself to something really nice to work at. It's just that when the delivery man got here and saw there was no lift, he refused to bring it up. Just left it here outside the building. What did he suppose I was going to do? Put it on my head and trot up to the second floor?"

"Well, do you want me to give you a hand to carry it upstairs?" Edward offered, dropping his rucksack at the side of the door.

"I hate to play the female in distress, but I just don't know whether I'll be able to help you there. And this is definitely a two man job." She slipped nimbly off the edge of the desk and danced over to where Edward had left his rucksack. "But I suppose we can give it a try." She set her handbag down carefully, before placing herself at the opposite end of the desk to Edward.

They both gripped the sides of the dark wood desk. "On a count of three," Rita said.

"One, two, three."

Edward's end went up easily enough. Rita got her end up, but after a few seconds she set it back down and shook her head. They hadn't moved a centimetre. "I'm sorry, I really don't think I can even carry it across to the stairs, let alone up them."

Edward slumped against the desk. "We'll have to get someone else to help."

In response to his comment, a mobile telephone started ringing. Rita hurried over to her handbag, flicking the lid back and pulling out a sleek black mobile. "Oh, it's a client," she groaned, recognising the number immediately. "I'd better take this."

Edward watched in awe as she answered the phone and transformed into a different person. She started to speak Chinese as if it were the most natural thing in the world. Casually, effortlessly. Certainly in appearance and demeanour she was the same, but the sounds coming from her lips were like nothing else. It wasn't just the alien words, but the rhythm and the tone of her speech that was so different. It was impossible to even judge the mood from the way she was speaking.

She talked for a few minutes, pausing now and then to listen to her client's requests. Nodding and saying something Edward couldn't understand, she hung up. Slipping the phone back in her handbag, she looked sheepishly over at Edward. "It's the curse of being freelance: people just presume you do nothing but work."

"That was Chinese?"

She nodded. "I'm a translator."

He was impressed. Edward had never been any good at languages at school, and had struggled enough with basic French. But from what he'd heard from people who knew something about linguistics, French was nothing compared to Chinese when it came to hard graft. Not only was there an alien bridge to gap of linguistic divide, but four tones and literally thousands of characters to learn.

"I'm impressed. You must have studied really hard to speak it that well. It sounded really fluent. Not that I speak Chinese…"

Rita smiled, a little embarrassed, and lowered her eyes for a moment. "It's not that impressive. My father's from China. I started very young."

"Rita!"

They both jumped. Oliver was striding up the footpath towards them.

"You moving the office outside in preparation for summer?"

"Not exactly." Rita smiled, a flirt in her eyes. "The delivery man refused to carry it upstairs. He just abandoned me out here with my desk." She paused, picking up her handbag, having already decided that she wouldn't need to try and help carry the desk anymore. "Orson, darling, do you think you and Edward will be able to manage to get this up to my flat?"

She didn't really leave either of them any option of refusal. Edward glanced over at Orson – so that was his name. Orson grinned at Rita. "We'll soon have it in its proper place."

"Oh, you boys – I can't thank you enough."

Between the two of them, they soon had the desk up the first section of stairs to the first floor. Edward could tell why the delivery man had refused. It was a very heavy desk – all that solid wood – and his arms were screaming. Taking a few moments to get a better grip on the desk and summon up another burst of brute force, Edward glanced back down the stairwell to the main doors. Rita was standing outside, arms folded and handbag caught in the crook of her arm. She had a lit cigarette caught elegantly between two fingers, but she wasn't smoking it, just staring off into the middle distance. A tight wisp of smoke curled up into the atmosphere. It was a captivating, silent, moody scene. Take a photograph in black and white, and she could have been Lauren Bacall or someone like that, Edward thought.

Toby didn't want to travel all the way up to the north of York. It would take at least two bus trips, he said, and he just couldn't be bothered. Besides, he had a date with one of the office temps. Edward could hear a girl giggling in the background.

It was bloody typical as far as Toby was concerned. Everything happened when and if it was suitable for him and what he wanted to do. He'd been the same at university but it hadn't been so noticeable then. There'd been more of the lads, and

Toby dropping the gang and picking them back up as and when hadn't mattered so much. They got along all right, and Toby was a good laugh, but he wasn't particularly missed when he didn't join in. Now the gang had disappeared and there was just Edward left, clutching a collection of South Korean zombie horror films that his brother, James had sent down for his younger sibling to sample. A lads' night in with beer and some gore had sounded good. On his own it just seemed a bit sad. Did people do things like this on their own? Edward wasn't sure. He'd spent the last few years constantly with the gang and fleeting girlfriends. He wasn't used to this much time on his own.

He would have asked Lexie if a night of nasty horror films appealed, but Lexie had gone funny the last couple of weeks. Edward had been here a month now – a whole month. At the start Lexie would have been up for a lads' night. Now she was more interested in calorie counting and exercising. She went to bed early because it helped with metabolism; even on a Friday night for crying out loud. She'd stopped drinking. So strong was her determination.

Underneath the desperate dieting, she had to be the same person, surely. Armed with his DVDs, Edward went downstairs to Lexie's flat.

The first change he noticed was that the modelling clay name plate was gone. The second was Lexie. Three weeks into her diet and exercise regime and the pounds had really started to shift. Her body was more toned. But it wasn't just that. Her style was changing, and the clothes she was beginning to wear made her look slimmer. This evening she was wearing a pair of properly fitting trousers and a blouse. She'd cut her hair. It was now shoulder length, with a fair amount of back combing to give it more volume.

"Lexie," he greeted her, a little surprised by the sudden changes. "You're looking really different."

"Aye, well," she shrugged, still seeming her old self, a little uncomfortable in her new skin. But wanting to settle in. "I'm turning twenty soon. Time to be growing up a bit, eh?"

"Right." He didn't know what else to say. "Listen, my brother sent me some horror DVDs. I was thinking about a night in; you know, few beers, a few nasty films. You up for that?"

"Oh no." Lexie shook her head, hair bouncing side to side. "I've got to stay off the booze, got a bit more to loose." She patted her stomach. "Anyway, I need an early night. I'm going to the gym tomorrow morning with Sophia."

The main entrance opened and the girl came in.

"Oh, hiya," Lexie said to her. "Haven't seen you about for a while."

The girl smiled politely. She couldn't take her eyes off Lexie, although she was trying not to look surprised by the transformation. "I'm either at work or language classes these days."

"You still learning the Dutch? You must be native by now."

"Almost."

"Oh, well. Thanks for the offer, Edward, but I'll have to pass this time. I'll be seeing you."

There was just Edward and the girl left in the entrance. Since that morning when they'd drank tea together after the screaming from Lexie's flat, he'd seen her a couple more times, always in her flat, and always drinking tea. They'd talked about this and that and nothing in particular and Edward still didn't know her name. The more times he saw her, the less he felt he could ask.

"What'cha got there?"

She usually wasn't so inquisitive. But the ice had gradually been breaking through those cups of tea. She was still a bit skittish, but he felt as though she was growing to trust him; like a wild bird coming to a human hand for food.

"These?" Edward held up the DVDs as if there could have been anything else she could have been referring to. "My brother sent them down for me to borrow. Korean zombie films. Thought I'd have a night in with a bit of blood and guts." He stopped jabbering. It was pointless asking, because she'd say no. But he could ask anyway. "That doesn't sound like anything for you?"

She considered the front cover of the DVD at the top of the pile. "Why not?"

"Really?" he coughed back his surprise.

"I never watch horror films usually. But I certainly don't see why a change wouldn't be a good idea."

"All right then. Let's go."

Getting the beers out of the fridge, he had to slap himself quickly to check this was reality. The girl was actually in his flat. The wisp of a creature who resembled some kind of ethereal fairy. Surely too far above everyday human pastimes such as horror films. Still, here she was.

"I was really surprised by Lexie," she said as she curled up on one end of his settee.

"It must be a recent change, I haven't seen her like that before."

"Do you know why she's doing it?"

He appeared in the living room doorway. "Doing what?"

"Changing her appearance."

"Oh. I think she's just wanting to be healthier." He shrugged. "Just waiting for the microwave to do its magic on the popcorn."

She didn't seem to hear him. "Do you know if she's doing it on her own?"

"How do you mean?"

"Is anyone helping her with her... dieting?"

"I don't know. I don't think so. Well, she said something about Sophia taking her to the gym tomorrow."

"Oh. I see." She looked rather sad at this news. "You know, before you moved in, Lexie was our most recent addition."

"Oh right, she's not been living here long?"

"Not that long."

"Beer?"

The girl stared at the offered can as if it were alien artefact. "I don't... I mean, I shouldn't really." She stopped then looked up and met his eye. "Why not?"

Edward grinned. "I'll go get the popcorn."

Because the flat smelt of wet laundry and something else he couldn't quite place, Edward decided to air his living space. Make it fresh and healthy. He had vague ideas of what to do, gleaned from memories of his mother and spring cleaning. Despite the good intentions, he was never going to be a self-sufficient man to make a domestic goddess proud. His first act was to fling the living room window open wide, knocking a row of books out in the process.

"Shit." He lent out of the window and peered out. At this side of the building there was a strip of lawn about two metres wide, then a boundary fence blocking off the next building's garden. His books were scattered over the grass, most of them open, spines creased and pages fluttering. But they hadn't taken any harm.

Outside, he scrambled like a tramp collecting rubbish, furtively picking up his books. He felt like an idiot, but there were some good sci-fi paperbacks in amongst all of these. He couldn't leave them for the birds.

A window close by opened. "What do you think you're doing?" a Northern Irish voice questioned.

Edward shot up, gathering an armful of books to him. A man was leaning out of the window of the ground floor flat, a half-smoked cigarette sticking out of the corner of his mouth in a nonchalant way. Edward gaped at the man, wondering if his eyes were deceiving him.

The man nodded at the books, ignoring Edward's stare.

"I knocked them out of my window," Edward explained.

The man nodded again, as if this was to be expected now and then. "You living in Kim's old place?"

"Kim?"

He raised his eyes as if about to pray.

"I live above you."

"That'd be the one." The man sucked the last glowing embers of life out of his cigarette and flicked it onto the lawn. He noticed Edward was still staring at him. "You still looking, kid?"

Edward tried to shake some sense into himself. Staring was rude; that was one of the things mother had always said. "I'm sorry. It's just that you really look like…"

"Yeah," the man agreed, sounding a little disgruntled. "It's the face, isn't it? A god damn curse, if you ask me. I think it's the only reason Sophia tolerates me. I used to work as a look-a-like, you know?"

"Humphrey Bogart."

"Aye, that's the one. But I'm not Bogie. I'm Ray O'Donnell."

"Do you still work as a look-a-like?" Edward was in awe of the man. He didn't really know much about films, and certainly not about the old black and white films. But Humphrey Bogart he knew because one of his flatmates in first year at university had insisted on pinning a giant poster of the icon in their shared living room.

"Na. Pain in the arse. I work in security these days. Not as much money in it, but I cover my needs. The rent's cheap here, especially for York, don't you think?"

"Yeah. When I was flat hunting I thought I'd have to go into a houseshare. This was a lot cheaper, affordable. But then it's out on the edge."

"That and they have to compensate, give you some incentive to stay. Besides, the landlady doesn't need the money."

Why so bitter, Edward wondered. But before he change to ask, Ray had nodded good day to him and shut the window. Now that he knew who was living in the flat above, conversation seemed pointless. So he cut it to an abrupt end. Edward remembered Lexie saying something about Ray being a bit unsociable, a bit odd. Back in the day before she'd gone a bit strange herself.

It was when he was running to get out of the flat and reach the bus stop in time that he saw the envelope. Brown and A5 in size, with nothing written on the front. It had been carefully sealed and pushed through his letterbox. It was too early for the postman and it definitely hadn't been there last night when he'd gone to bed.

Edward glanced across at it as he tied his shoelaces. What was this supposed to be? It was all a bit twee. Although he doubted it was something exciting. Just a circular to all local households – either advertising or a letter from a charity begging for donations. He threw the envelope into his rucksack and hurried out of the flat.

The girl was waiting at the bus stop. She had a green tweed coat on with big round buttons. Clutching a spotted shoulder bag in front of her like a proper little school girl. Her hair was even in pig tails. She smiled at him with those big, dusky eyes.

"Morning," he panted, running across the road to the bus stop.

She nodded up the road. "Just in time."

The bus came around the corner, the indicator flashing as the driver saw the two figures waiting. They got on, showing the driver their four week passes. Edward followed the girl up the aisle and sat down next to her just as the bus pulled away.

"You survived our Korean zombie night, then?"

She smiled lightly. "I've seen worse. Besides, it's fun to be a little scared sometimes, isn't it?"

"Certainly is." Although in her case, it had seemed as though the films had actually made her relax. After the first scream, something was forgotten, and she had been the most comfortable he had ever seen her. But this morning she was back to her polite and withdrawn stance. So light and fragile that if the wind blew hard she might just disappear.

It wasn't until the middle of the morning, bored with his current assignment, that he remembered the brown envelope. Junk mail would be a welcome distraction from work. He was in a corner cubicle and no one would notice.

Unzipping the rucksack, he quickly found the envelope. Ripping open the top, he pulled out the contents – a single sheet of folded white paper. Charity begging letter, he guessed. But when he unfolded it, he saw that it was actually a photocopy of part of a page from a newspaper. The top right hand corner of the newspaper had come through on the copy, showing the date to be a few months prior.

Edward smoothed the sheet out on his desk, not understanding why someone would send him this.

And send it anonymously. It wasn't even clear which piece he was supposed to be looking at. There was part of an article about a piglet wearing wellington boots; an advert for a dry cleaners; an article about a woman's body being pulled from the River Ouse and a piece about some road safety features that were to be added to a residential area in one of the suburbs.

Why did he want this?

He read over the article about the dead body – at least that sounded promising. Police divers had found the body of a twenty-four year old woman called Judy Polwart the previous afternoon. An investigation was continuing. The police were waiting for an autopsy report. Judy had been missing for five days. Family and friends had said that she had been out of sorts and depressed the last few months. Sounded like a suicide to him. And one that had occurred several months ago now. Why should he care about this?

Crumpling up the sheet, he stuffed it back into his rucksack. If he was going to get caught avoiding work, it might as well be for something worth while.

One evening there was a stack of post waiting for Edward when he got home for work. Not one was addressed to him bar a telephone bill. Flicking through the envelopes, he saw they were all for the same person. Postman obviously couldn't be arsed to sort out the building's post.

Mr A. Leach. Mr Archibald Leach. It was funny, he knew that Archie must be an abbreviation of the name Archibald, but he'd never thought of Archie as actually being an Archibald. It sounded like such an antiquated name. Belonging to another century. Although considering it wasn't that long ago that it was the twentieth century, that really wasn't saying so much.

Edward went up the two flights of stairs to the top floor. He was just about to push the letters through the letterbox when the door opened.

"Edward," Archie exclaimed. "Why are you creeping outside my door?"

Feeling foolish, Edward straightened and handed over the letters. "I got your post."

"Ah, spreading the good news?" Archie said eagerly. His face dropped slightly as he checked over the envelopes, guessing where each one had come from. "Or perhaps not so good. So how are you settling in?"

"Fine."

"Drink that bourbon yet?"

Edward winced. Archie looked so pleased with himself; he didn't have the heart to tell him that it was still stood unopened in the kitchen cupboard. "I've made a start on it," he lied.

"Great stuff," he enthused. "Whilst I have you here, I need to tell you that it's Lexie's birthday next week. Turning twenty. No longer a teenager."

"Oh right."

"We're having a little get together next Friday. Nothing too formal. We'll probably go out to dinner later. But to start off, it's cocktails here at half six. Shall we see you then?"

Saying no didn't feel like an option. "Of course. Thanks for the invite, Archie."

"Good man." Archie patted him on the back. "I'll see you then. In the meantime, you'll have to excuse me. I'm in the middle of a fascinating documentary about energy production in Iceland. Absolutely amazing what they get up to over there. You wouldn't believe it."

Edward probably wouldn't have. Archie returned to the television. Edward went back downstairs and cracked open the bourbon.

Edward travelled up to Durham that weekend to visit his parents. He had never suffered from homesickness before, and certainly at university he had only ever returned during the holidays, always with that suitcase full of dirty laundry. Increasingly since moving to York he'd been feeling lost and rootless. Getting used to working full time and living on your own in a town where you didn't really know anyone wasn't as easy as you might have thought. He needed a change of scene. A little reminder of who he was.

He took the train up to Durham and a bus out to his parents' semi-detached. His father was sat in the kitchen planting spring bulbs into boxes for the base of the windows, as he did every year.

"Edward!" his father greeted him as he came in through the back door. "I wasn't expecting to see you."

"Just thought I'd come up and see you all." He set his rucksack by the washing machine.

"That's not full of dirty socks, I hope."

"No, just a few things for the night."

His father nodded and put another bulb into compost. There was an awkward silence. His father was wondering why his son was visiting. But he couldn't really work it out and he really couldn't put it into words, so it was just better to keep quiet.

"Mum about?"

"Oh yes. She's through in the living room. Glued to that new DVD player every weekend these days. Having her nostalgia trips."

Was his father jealous of a DVD player? Edward watched his silent father plant bulbs. "Right. I'll just pop through and say hello." What had he been hoping for? A brass band to welcome him home; signs that life had come to a halt whilst he had been away and only now could people dry their tears and get on with their lives?

His mother was sat in the living room watching television.

"Hello, Mum."

She twisted around, a look of pleasant surprise. "Edward! What are you doing back?"

"Just thought I'd come up and see how you're all doing." He stood awkwardly in the living room, staring at the television screen. Men in suits were dancing with women in large skirts, curled hair and ribbons. "What are you watching?"

"*Gone with the Wind*. I haven't seen this film for years."

Edward sat down on the settee beside her.

"Did you come up for any special reason?"

He shook his head. "Just came for a visit."

She nodded and turned back to the television. "Your brother James was the same in the beginning. Felt unsettled. I think he used to come back just to check we were still here. Soon got settled in. I think finding that girlfriend helped. Mind you, that's all over now."

Edward sat and watched the rest of the film with his mother. They all had lunch together in the kitchen. His father went out to a garden centre in the afternoon. Edward and his mother went to watch another film. This one was called *Mogambo*; he didn't really get it: something about two silly women running after some swarthy man's man in Africa. Still, it seemed to entertain his mother.

Before dinner he went up to his old bedroom with his rucksack. Sat down on the single bed and stared at the posters from his teenage years. The box of wooden toys from his childhood. There was a stack of textbooks and ringbinder files full of lecture notes in the wardrobe. Remnants from his student days. Already it was just another memory to be boxed up and left in storage at his parents' house.

And now he was Edward the adult. Embarking on his grown-up life, his career and everything else. Somehow he didn't really feel old enough for it.

PART TWO

"Edward!"

Edward smiled sheepishly. In anyone else such enthusiasm would have seemed sarcastic, but Archie always appeared to be genuinely thrilled about everything. He had a joy for life rarely seen.

Loitering outside Archie's door, clutching his feeble offering for Lexie's twentieth – a selection of inoffensive bubblebaths. He'd wondered about chocolates, but then remembered she was on a diet. In his smart jeans and his 'going-out' shirt; Archie had said it was nothing too formal. But when Archie opened door, Edward felt a lead weight drop down in his stomach. Archie was wearing a suit. How was this informal?

If Archie noted Edward's very informal dress, he showed nothing on his face. "Just in time. Come in and we'll get you sorted with something to drink."

Edward stepped into the flat, hoping Archie just had the wrong idea of what informal was, but looking around the room, he realised it was he who was out of place.

"Edward, you came!" a peroxide-blonde woman in a full-length slinky pink dress shuffled up to him as fast as her tight skirts would allow. She had fake eyelashes on, giving her a slightly sleepy appearance, and her styled and volumised hair had a look that she'd just stumbled out of bed. It wasn't until she went for the present that he realised she was Lexie.

"You got me a present, how sweet!" she exclaimed.

Edward stared incredulously at her. Realised he hadn't seen her for quite a while now. "Jesus, Lexie," he exclaimed. "You've lost some weight," he blurted out without thinking. Either it was extreme weight loss or the effect of ditching the toothpaste jeans and switching over to the ball dress.

Lexie giggled and clutched her unopened present. "I know. It's great. The people at work hardly recognise me. I'll just go give Archie a hand."

Abandoned again, Edward stepped to the side of the room, feeling distinctly underdressed and out of place.

At the window, which was wide open, Ray O'Donnell and Orson were talking. Ray, dressed in a dark suit and leaning against the window sill in a nonchalant way, cigarette hanging between two fingers with a trail of smoke lazily drifting outside, looking even more like Bogart than he had done the other day. Orson sucked on his own cigarette and nodded in agreement to something Ray had just said.

Jazz music played in the background. Edward's eyes wandered. Rita was retiring on the settee, a cocktail glass in one hand. She was wearing a sleeveless evening dress like a giant sheet of indigo silk casually wrapped around her frame. She caught his eye and smiled a greeting.

"Rita," he nodded to her. "Desk going all right?"

Rita tilted her head back; the cascade of waved hair slipping off her shoulder. "Oh, it's just perfect. We've tried it out, haven't we?" she added, catching Orson's eye.

Orson grinned at her. Edward got the feeling they weren't talking about work anymore.

"Edward, wonderful to see you here." Sophia appeared by his side, like the hostess even though this wasn't her flat. She was a little more casually dressed than the others, in a full-skirted halterneck dress, but she still managed to make Edward feel very out of place. "Did you have a nice week at work?"

Nice? It didn't feel like a word that could match up with work. He was certainly accustomed to going into the office five days a week to the point where it didn't feel like he'd ever done anything else with his life. It wasn't particularly inspiring, and he always had one eye on the clock whilst he was there. It was quite depressing to think this was going to be it till he hit sixty-five.

Edward shrugged. "It's just work."

Sophia nodded. "I do think it's quite hard to get into work you actually enjoy."

Archie reappeared, passing Edward a drink. Edward stared down at the cut glass tumbler. The drink looked like whisky on ice. Archie was certainly keen on his spirits; had no one ever told him about beer?

"So what's the plan for tonight?"

"We're going into town to a restaurant," Sophia answered. "I've got the taxis arriving soon. In fact," she paused, glancing over the room. "Now that we're all here, perhaps we ought to go down soon."

Archie surveyed the room, then waggled his finger at Sophia. "You know we're not all here."

Sophia sighed audibly loud and rolled her eyes. "Why bother? She won't want to join us." She folded her arms and looked like a sulky child.

"Now, now dear," Archie scolded her patiently. "We all know you're more generous than that. I'll go down and fetch her." He gave her a kiss on the cheek and then was gone.

Out of the building, there was only the girl missing. Edward hadn't expected to see her here; somehow she didn't exist within this community as a whole. More like a frightened animal who was always there in the background, as if it couldn't quite get away.

Five minutes later Archie returned, his arm around the girl's waist; gently leading her into the flat. She looked bashful, not entirely comfortable with having been persuaded to come up. When she looked over in Sophia's direction she looked scared. She ought to have been chilling out on a Friday night, but even the girl was dressed more in keeping with the crowd than Edward was. She had a green, long and full-bodied skirt on; a smart white shirt with pointed collar, and a neat little scarf tied around her neck. Her hair was pinned up on the back of her head.

Two black cab taxis arrived promptly to pick the party up, lining up efficiently outside the flats. Edward waited and watched as Lexie, Rita, Orson and Archie got into the first taxi, one after the other, all stunningly dressed as if they were off to a film premiere.

The odd group was left to take the final taxi: the out of place, the terrified, the belligerent and the grumpy. The girl was first in, virtually pressing herself to the window like one of those stuffed animals you see suckered in on passenger door windows. She didn't say a word for the entire journey. Ray was next, grumbling that he was starving. Then Edward, and finally Sophia. Checking her make up in a compact out of her handbag, Sophia didn't speak much on the journey into town, but Edward was very aware of being cramped in next to her; the heat of her body, the almost over-powering scent of her perfume.

When they got into town, Ray took the girl in hand, taking her arm and leading her down the road after Archie, Lexie, Rita and Orson; telling her not to mind these idiots. Edward hung back, watching the glamorous procession and feeling like an alien. He really didn't belong with these people.

"Edward, are you all right?"

Sophia appeared by his side like a fairy godmother. She followed his gaze down the pedestrianised street where their neighbours walked, jumping from one figure to the next. "What did Archie tell you about the party?"

"What?"

"Well, did he tell you anything about the dress code?"

"Dress code?" Edward laughed awkwardly. "You make it sound serious."

Sophia chirruped out a laugh. Pulled her wrap around her shoulders. "Of course it's not serious, it's a party. It's supposed to be fun. But you seem uncomfortable."

"Archie said it was casual."

Sophia nodded, understanding. "And one man's casual is another man's formal."

"I stick out like a sore thumb."

"Look, darling," Sophia started, almost scolding him for his lack of confidence. "They're just clothes. Of course, they're wearing stylish, well-chosen garments, and they do look fantastic. But that doesn't make them better people than you. It just makes them people who have bought some good clothes. You do understand that, don't you?"

"I suppose so," Edward muttered, wondering if her little speech was actually supposed to make him feel better about himself.

"I know!" Sophia clapped her hands in excitement. "I'll show you anyone can do this. Next weekend."

"What about next weekend?"

"I'm taking you shopping," she replied, taking him decidedly by the arm and marching him after the others. "I work in fashion, remember? I can make you into one of the most stylish men in York. Don't you worry about a thing."

Lexie was really drunk. She had been chattering about nothing at Edward and Rita all the way home in the taxi. She was still talking to Edward now, having followed him into his flat. Edward hoped she wasn't expecting to sleep with him. As much as he liked her, he really didn't like her in that way.

Amorous seduction seemed to be the last thing on her mind as she staggered in his living room. Switching on the television. "Come on, Edward," she waved her arms, seeming more like the Lexie he had hung out with when first moving in here; less like the glamour star she had become. "Let's watch television. I'm a proper adult now, twenty years old. I can stay up as long as I like."

"I think you've been doing that a while now."

Lexie laughed. "Oh aye, but I'm no teenager now, am I?"

Edward shrugged. It was three o'clock in the morning but he didn't feel tired. "Sure, do what you like. I'm just going to check my email."

Lexie watched him sit down at the little computer desk in the corner of the living room.

"You boys and your computers," she drawled, flopping down onto the settee. One of her high-heeled sandals fell off and clattered to the floor. "I've never really seen the attraction, although the Internet is very useful."

"Yeah." Edward wasn't really paying attention; hypnotised by the artificial glow of the screen on his face. He'd got broadband in the flat and the computer connected to the Internet immediately. There wasn't anything interesting in his hotmail account. Shouldn't really expect anything better for three in the morning. Something from his brother, James; and something from Toby that looked like it would be lewd from what the subject header promised. He was aware of Lexie humming in the background.

"Anything good?"

He clicked out of hotmail. "No."

Lexie was spinning one of her sandals round on a finger, rather inelegantly. Edward watched her, feeling the room slope forwards. He had probably drunk a bit too much. At least he didn't have to get up for work in a few hours.

Lexie giggled. "Look at me. Dressed up all lady like. My mother would have a fit."

"I'll tell you what," Edward said as he went to the kitchen. "I didn't recognise you this evening."

"What, I'm usually scruffy?" she snorted. She tilted her head back on the arm of the settee. "Is that the fridge I hear? Can I get a beer?"

"I thought you were watching the weight."

"Oh aye, I'll be exercising tomorrow again. Or today. Tomorrow is today." She started giggling. "But either way it's my birthday."

Edward returned to the living room with a couple of cans. He really shouldn't drink this one last beer, but his thoughts were too weighted down in the suds of late-night silliness and he couldn't let her drink alone.

Lexie dragged at the ringpull on the can. There was a hiss as it opened. "You're right though, I do look very different. Finally growing up. Sophia said I resemble my namesake more and more every day." She sat upright in a prim pose as she said the last sentence, her eyelids drooping. "God, that computer's bright."

"Your namesake? Who else is Lexie?" Edward slumped back into the settee. "What's that short for again?"

"Alexandra." Lexie dropped her sandals and tottered over to the computer. "Can I google something?"

He waved his arms out expansively. "Be my guest."

"Let's have a wee look here."

"So who is it you resemble? Who is Alexandra? Alexander the Great?"

"Who?"

He glanced over at her, hoping she was joking, or just too drunk to remember anything she knew. Lexie was perched at the computer table, her face lit up by the screen. Her lips seemed very red.

"She meant my surname."

"Your second name? What's that then? MacDonald?"

"No."

"MacDuff?"

"No," she drawled.

"MacIntosh?"

"Edward, do you think everyone from Scotland is a Mac?"

"They're certainly a something."

She rolled her eyes – more than words could say. "I'm a Monroe."

"Monroe?"

"Yes. Look at this." She typed something into the computer then clicked the mouse a couple of times. Turning the computer screen, she directed the full-screen image at Edward, then struck a similar pouting pose.

Edward started laughing. "Oh yes, you and Marilyn Monroe, you two could be sisters."

The noise was infectious. Lexie started laughing. She took another drink of beer, but was laughing too much to swallow. It bubbled back up through her nose. "Oh man," she gasped, wiping her face with the back of her hand. "I can't see Marilyn doing this."

"Behind closed doors, you never know."

"True." She slouched back in the computer chair. "You know, I reckon I could be glamorous."

Edward raised his beer can. "You were very glamorous tonight."

"A proper Monroe," Lexie mused. "Wouldn't it have been funny if my mother had called me Marilyn."

"Mad is what it would have been."

"I could do it," she muttered, sitting up to type something in the computer.

"What are you doing now?"

Lexie suddenly screamed and clapped her hands together. "Oh my god, it was right. You can do it online. Come and look!"

Edward rolled off the settee and staggered to the computer. "Look at what?"

"You can change your name on line."

"Is this one of those crappy things that makes numbers out of your name and tells you who you're going to marry?"

"Is that where you go when you're lonely, eh, Edward?" Lexie joked.

"Yeah, right," he sniffed, peering closely at the screen as if short sighted. "This looks official."

"It is. Change your name by deed poll online."

"No."

She looked up at him, grinning wickedly. "Do you dare me?"

"It can't be that simple."

"I could be Marilyn Monroe when I wake up."

"If that's the case, how can you not?"

"Exactly." Lexie clicked on to the next page. "Life's here for living."

On Wednesday Edward swore he didn't want his job anymore. This wasn't a graduate training scheme; it was a soul-destroying sentence in a torture factory.

After two months, there were elements of his job that he still didn't understand, but his more experienced colleagues never seemed to have the time to explain anything to him. There wasn't a manual or office procedures guide that he had found. He tried his best to use his initiative and muddle along, but there were times when, short of being telepathic, he could go no further. It never seemed to be enough.

Right now he was staring another piece of frustration in the face but it wasn't backing down. Work allocation. He'd asked one of his colleagues, a forty something woman with sharp little eyes and dyed mahogany hair. He'd just asked for advice. He'd never said he knew everything.

The woman scowled and threw her pen loudly onto her desk, hoping he would take the hint. She was trying to work and idiots were disturbing her. "I thought you were supposed to be the graduate."

"I am."

"Well, go use that degree level brain and figure it out. Or it is more used to working out philosophy than real life?"

He hadn't even studied philosophy as an extra at university. The woman got up and stormed somewhere important. If Edward had been sharper or had a little more self-confidence, he would have made some fitting comment at this point. Just because she had a hang up about the fact that she hadn't gone to university – and it was very clear from her vocalised opinion on all graduates that she wasn't one of the group – it didn't mean he should have to put up with such unprofessional behaviour. But Edward was still new to the world of work, and words failed him. He stood awkwardly with his task in hand, feeling pathetic. Looked around the office and was horrified at what he saw.

No one seemed to have even noticed her outburst. People typed at their computers, made notes on papers, had quiet conversations and continued the business of the office. No one had even glanced at him. Surely the office gossips would not be so unobservant as to miss such an opportunity. But there was absolutely nothing. Edward raised his hand, the sheet of paper held up like a white flag.

"Can anyone give us a hand?"

Anyone and everyone ignored him. He might as well have been invisible.

He got home that evening to discover that more anonymous papers had been pushed through his letterbox. This time it was a missing person's poster. He'd glanced over it, wondering if she lived in the area, until he noticed the name, Judy Polwart, and realised that it was the name in the newspaper article that had been hand delivered to his flat. This wasn't a recent poster; it was several months old: crinkled, now redundant. It was public knowledge what had happened to Judy Polwart. She was dead.

Edward wandered into the kitchen and put the A4 poster on the work top. Judy Polwart, aged twenty-four. Curious that she was so young, because looking at the photograph, her hair looked positively white. A grey, silvery white carefully styled and pinned up. It had to be dyed, he thought to himself, looking at those eyebrows. Very dark, and incredibly high and arching. Something had to be faked. And she definitely didn't look particularly old. He peered at the unfamiliar face. Why does someone want me to have your missing poster? I don't know you. I never missed you.

Someone was hammering on the door.

"Edward?"

It was Lexie.

She pushed her way into the flat as soon as he opened the door. She was red in the face, hot, angry.

She waved torn envelopes and official looking letters at him.

"I've only gone and bloody done it!" she yelled, thrusting the paperwork at him, delegating him as responsible, and marching into the living room.

Edward watched her flop onto the settee. "What's up with you?"

"Do you remember Friday night?"

"Your birthday party? Yeah, it was a good night."

"Do you remember what we did when we came back to yours?" she hissed.

Edward paled. He didn't remember sleeping with Lexie. He didn't want to either; not now, not in the future and definitely not in the past. He didn't want to be mixed up in Toby's past conquests, and besides which, Lexie was like a sibling. He had had a lot to drink on Friday though, and he couldn't actually remember going to bed. Was she going to tell him she was pregnant?

"You needn't look so terrified, hen," she said sarcastically. "It's not you who's in trouble."

Oh Christ, she was pregnant.

"Are you going to keep it?"

"Keep it?" she howled. "It's done now, what choice do I have?"

Edward was going to be sick.

"You just take a look at that letter," Lexie told him. "I can't believe you let me do it. It was supposed to be a laugh. I don't want to actually change my name."

"Change your name?" His heart thudded hopefully against his rib cage. She wasn't pregnant. They hadn't slept together. He'd passed out on the settee. After playing on the computer. After being on the Internet. After changing Lexie's name on deed poll.

He looked down at the letter she'd given him. "Christ, you really have applied to change your name."

The letter was addressed to Alexandra Monroe, but it was in regards to a new woman, the next Marilyn Monroe. Edward started to laugh. "I never thought I'd end up living upstairs from Marilyn Monroe."

"Don't laugh. It's really not funny. How can I be called Marilyn? That's no' my name. I'm Lexie," she finished aggressively.

He flicked through the sheets. "You still are."

"No I'm not. That's from deed poll or whoever they are."

"I know, but this is just an application," Edward explained, passing her the letter back. "Even the government wouldn't be stupid enough to let you make a big change like that online. How would they even know it was you who was wanting to make the change?"

Lexie meekly took the letters back. "I suppose. I didn't really read it properly. I panicked a bit when I saw it was from deed poll."

"You got to fill in all that, sign it, and send in documents. You've got to prove to them that you really are who you say you are and that you really want to go ahead with this."

"So if I don't reply to this…"

"Then you're still Lexie."

She nodded resolutely. "Well, that's all right then."

"Just make sure you destroy those letters," Edward grinned. "You wouldn't want to fill the forms in on another drunken whim."

"You are not funny."

The girl didn't understand why it was all actually very funny, especially the part about Lexie believing she really was Marilyn Monroe, when Edward told her about it a few days later. They were walking on Strensall Common, an area of low lying heath to the north of York. Owned by the MOD but open to the public most of the time for walking, it was a curious windblown, open landscape that looked like it was a large upland area but was actually low lying at the base of the Yorkshire Wolds. There was something almost endless about it; far removed from the rest of the civilised world.

She stopped walking and stared intensely at Edward. "She changed her name to Marilyn Monroe?"

"She just applied online. It was last Friday, she'd had a bit too much to drink."

"But she's not Marilyn?"

"No, no, no. You've got to do a bit more than play about online to make it official. She got all the forms through in the post and panicked. She didn't bother to read the letter properly and thought her name had already been changed. You should have seen her face."

She wasn't very interested in Lexie's face. The wind blew across them, whipping her loose hair away from her face like a stream of fire. "Has she destroyed the letter?"

"Oh, don't worry, she's not going to become Marilyn."

"But you saw her destroy the letter?"

"Well, no," Edward faltered, not really recalling what had happened to the letter. It didn't seem important. "But she won't be replying."

The girl wrapped her arms around her body and started walking again. "I just hope she's ripped it up. Ripped it into a thousand pieces."

Why so serious? She had looked horrified, as if someone had died. Edward shook it from his mind. The girl had a funny way about her. Normal rules of interpretation of behaviour couldn't always be applied to her. She probably just couldn't understand why anyone might want to apply to change their name to Marilyn Monroe for a joke.

Edward glanced uncertainly at the racks of expensive looking dresses, and wondered if this was to be an elaborate practical joke.

This was most definitely a woman's clothing boutique. Small, independent, and with nothing to offer the modern man; unless of course he was interested in a bit of cross-dressing on a weekend. What the hell was Edward doing here?

He stepped across to the shop front. Peering out between the full skirts of the window display – they seemed to be going for a 50s theme at the moment – he stared out onto the medieval narrow street of York, now converted as best as anyone could for modern consumerism. Tourists ambled slowly down the street, gazing up at the buildings and getting in the way of locals now blind to the historical architecture.

"Edward."

He jumped. Sophia had her hands on her hips. She had a smile on her face, but somehow there was an aggressive demeanour about her. As long as he did as bidden, everything would be all right.

This was the shop that Sophia managed. She didn't always come in on Saturdays, and usually left those weekends in the care of her well-styled deputy: the woman with secretary glasses and carefully waved blonde hair stood at the cash desk. Between the two, the intense air of dominating female efficiency was stifling.

"Mr Chin is ready for you now."

Who the hell was Mr Chin? Edward looked uncertainly at her but didn't move. "I think we've got our wires crossed, Sophia," he told her cautiously. "I thought you were just going to take me to M&S."

Sophia laughed out loud. Her deputy smiled at him in a pitying way.

"Oh Edward," Sophia sighed. "M&S is all very well for the basics, and for when you're shopping on your own in a rush. But every man needs a really good suit."

"I don't mind their suits."

"I mean tailoring." Sophia pursed her lips.

Edward felt ill. "You mean custom made?" He wasn't going to be able to afford this. Just what kind of graduate training scheme did she think he'd gotten a placement on?

She nodded. "Tailoring."

"I can't afford this."

"You can," she retorted, her Italian vowels getting a touch impatient. "Edward, you have to trust me on this," she continued, taking his arm and leading him to the fitting rooms at the back of the property. "Proper tailoring can make such a difference. We're all the same underneath, but get a good, properly fitting and stylishly cut piece of clothing and suddenly you're someone else. You said you felt uncomfortable at Marilyn's birthday party. The reason you felt uncomfortable was tailoring. I know it will cost a little bit more than taking something off the rack at a big chain store, but it's worth it to get something that's just right. It will do wonders for your self esteem."

"Sophia, I really don't have a lot of money at the moment…"

"You worry too much. Besides, you're not paying UK prices. You'll be paying Indian prices."

Mr Chin was a small man with nimble fingers, a polite and reserved manner and an eagerness for his work. Originally from Hong Kong, he had moved to India ten years ago and ran an exclusive tailoring business: hand made suits for the gentleman who knew exactly what he wanted. Most of his customers came to him, but every so often he would travel to different parts of the world, have a couple of days in some exhibition centre taking hundreds of measurements and orders. He'd then fly home, get the suits made and shipped out. Everyone was happy.

Sophia had first met Mr Chin through Archie several years ago. Mr Chin had been to London this week for one such order session, and was taking a short trip up through the UK to Edinburgh, stopping off at historical cities on the way. Sophia had asked for a special favour, and Mr Chin assured Edward that it would be his suit that would be made first when he returned home.

Sophia chattered about fabrics and colours as Mr Chin took the minutest of measurements; Edward standing in the middle like a dummy. Feeling like a child playing at grown-ups. Daring to meet his own gaze in the full-length mirrors every so often and asking himself what on earth he'd agreed to.

Mr Chin was stood beside him, tape measure around his neck, making notes in a small pad. Chinese symbols that could have meant anything. Perhaps nothing to do with the construction of this mythical suit and more to do with Edward's unsuitability to be dressed so finely.

Mr Chin snapped his leather bound notebook shut and looked up at Edward. "You pay deposit now." He handed a small slip of paper.

Edward looked at the figure. "This is the deposit?" he asked, horrified. "How much is this going to be?"

Sophia slapped his arm. "Don't be so rude. Mr Chin is an internationally renowned tailor. You are getting this at a special price. If you went to any of the tailors in London you'd have to pay at least twice that amount."

Edward begrudgingly wrote out a cheque, feeling he couldn't do anything but; especially considering the man had taken a pause in his holiday to take this particular order. There was a deal of politeness and compliments between Sophia and Mr Chin, then the tailor was gone.

"Well now." Sophia stepped up behind Edward and they both stared into the full-length mirror. Sophia looked like the glamorous Italian woman she was. Edward still had that look of awkward youth about him, reasonably tall, thin but with broadening shoulders, closely cropped dark hair. He still looked like he needed to grow into himself.

Sophia appraised him. "Have you ever thought about growing your hair a little longer?"

"I'm not really into grunge."

Sophia laughed. "I didn't mean that long. Just a couple of inches. You could give it a little more style." She tapped a finger thoughtfully to her chin. "You could grow a moustache."

Edward snorted. "I'd look like a German porn star."

"Nonsense. It would make you look a little older. Much more masculine."

"In completely the wrong way."

She ignored him. Picking up her handbag, she walked back out into the boutique. "Come along. We're going to look at shoes now. I'm afraid we'll have to go to the highstreet for those."

Shoes? Oh Christ, he groaned inwardly, following her out of the shop. This was going to take all day.

After shoes and a very long lecture on ties, Sophia declared it was enough for the morning. They needed lunch. It was half one and Edward's stomach had been making enough noise to suggest it was about to start self-digesting.

"I know a wonderful little Italian," she said, taking Edward's arm again.

For a moment he worried she was going to take him to another small tailor.

Walking up a snicket towards Parliament Street, they met Toby and a girl Edward didn't know coming in the opposite direction. The girl looked very young, probably some office junior at the place Toby worked. Toby liked to go for younger girls most of the time, especially silly ones. He liked to feel superior.

"Edward!" Toby shouted as if there was any possibility they hadn't been seen. "Long time no see!"

The two couples slowed down as they met. Toby looked at Sophia with surprise, his mind working through the possibilities. Toby never had had much imagination. Besides, he was a little upset that Edward might have succeeded where he had failed. "Got yourself a sugar-mommy, then?"

The girl with Toby – he never bothered to introduce her – giggled.

Sophia stared down her nose at Toby. "What a rude little boy you are."

Toby looked a little taken aback that people who looked like Sophia still talked like that these days. "Little boy? What the…"

Sophia flashed him an insincere smile, interrupting him before the swearing started up. "It was so nice to see you. Do get in touch again when you've grown up."

Edward stumbled after her as she marched up towards Parliament Street. There was a distinct air of slapped silence, no one really knowing what kind of retort was suitable for what she'd just said. There was definitely something about her mannerism and the way she said things that set her apart from other people.

"I don't think I've ever seen anyone get the last word with Toby," Edward told her, a little in awe.

"Yes, well," Sophia muttered, pausing at the corner. A little irritated, trying to calm herself down, she took a compact out of her handbag and reapplied her lipstick. "I'm not just anyone."

Edward continued to suffer from outbursts of female tempers. A week later Lexie had no real cause to attack him, and yet she did so regardless. After another week of feeling like the unwanted party at work, he didn't need that kind of grief from his neighbours. He was starting to wonder if there was something wrong with him. Something about him that said punchbag.

They had collided on Haxby mainstreet. To many intents and purposes, Haxby was just northern sprawl of York, separated off from the encroaching city by a mere ring road. And yet it still had retained its sense of being its own entity, harking back to a time soon to be swallowed up in modern suburban living. The village's main street, lined with trees, short and sweet served only an over grown village and yet it had its own post office, supermarkets and various banks. It seemed almost too much for the population.

Edward had wandered down in search of a change of scene. He also needed to buy and post a birthday card to his mother in the hope that he wouldn't miss her birthday the coming Monday. He didn't really feel like sitting in the flat, but didn't want to go into town either, and had settled on an aimless wander. It was in front of the memorial hall, a red bricked building that looked like a Victorian school house, that he collided with Lexie.

She looked harassed. Probably late for work. Her work shirt wasn't tucked into her trousers, her name tag dangling askew and threatening to drop off. Her hair looked slept in, volumised and tangled. She was sleepy, and to compensate and cover up, she had applied heavy eye shadow and eyeliner.

Her eyes narrowed when she saw Edward, and she walked even faster. Her bag was gaping open, dangling on the crook of her elbow as if it had desperately jumped up for the ride as Lexie was leaving for work. She was rooting through the contents for something.

"You!" she shouted at him, the Glaswegian sounding particularly aggressive that morning. "You told me I didn't need to worry."

Oh Christ, what now? Edward slowed, stepping to the side of the footpath and somehow hoping she'd just storm straight past him. He had the feeling this wasn't really going to be his responsibility and yet he was about to take all the blame.

Lexie waved a brown envelope in his face. "You said it was nothing to worry about and now look what's landed in the post today."

"Lexie, I…"

"Look at it!" she demanded.

Edward gingerly opened the torn envelope and looked inside. A few pieces of paper and a little book. He glanced up at Lexie, then back into the envelope before taking it out. It was a British passport. "I don't understand. Are you going on holiday?"

"Holiday?" Lexie screeched. "You think I'd dare go on holiday on that?"

"The photo?" Edward guessed. "Everyone thinks their passport photo is rubbish, I wouldn't worry about it." He flicked through the empty pages to the identification page at the back. The photograph didn't look all that bad, actually. He held it up and compared it with the furious image of Lexie. It was a recent picture, with her beach, bleach blonde hair in the styled and curled bob she had chosen to go with.

"It's not the picture," she told him tightly. "It's the name."

"The name?" He glanced at the details. Marilyn Monroe. "Shit," he burst out without thinking. "Is this a real passport?"

"Yes," Lexie snapped, watching him flick back through it all. "I'm getting paperwork through as I've changed my name to Marilyn."

"Why did you do a thing like that?"

"I didn't!" she shouted. People walking on the other side of the road looked over at them. "Why the hell would I want to be called Marilyn Monroe? But I am now. Do you know I have to pay to change my name back? Do you know how much passports cost these days?"

"But you must have paid…"

"I didn't do a thing!" Lexie stubbornly persisted. "This must be a free service when you first change your name."

"Don't be daft."

"Don't you tell me what to do," she snapped, snatching her new passport back. "It's your fault that I'm in this mess now. You told me that I didn't need to worry when I got that letter."

"Well, you didn't need to. You did destroy the letter, didn't you?"

Lexie scowled. "I threw it away," she said avoiding his eye. "And I certainly didn't ask for this. This is all your fault, you know?"

"I am not responsible for this. You would have had to have filled in forms and paid up money for your passport. It's got a recent photo of you in it, for crying out loud."

"Don't bandy logic with me. I haven't got the time for this. I'm already late for work."

"Right." Edward glanced down at her name tag. "Will you be changing your name tag for work as well?" He knew he shouldn't, be he couldn't resist.

Lexie swore at him and marched haughtily off to work.

It was ridiculous that she was blaming him. Who on earth could get a new passport without having signed a form or sent off a cheque? Who on earth would even attempt to suggest such a thing were possible? It sounded just like the kind of dizzy blonde antics you'd expect from someone like Marilyn Monroe, he decided in conclusion as he snapped shut the book of Dutch grammar he had been thumbing through without understanding a thing.

The girl glanced around from the washing up.

"I don't see why she had to blame me."

"You told her she didn't need to worry."

"Well, she didn't!" he protested. "She must have applied for that passport. It is a funny going on, though. Can you believe it, someone actually applying to be called Marilyn Monroe?" He lent back in the chair and contemplated the sunset out of the window. "Funny thing is, she's starting to look like her as well."

The girl sighed in exasperation and sank her hands deep into the washing up bubbles. "Oh, Edward. How can you be so stupid?"

Who killed Kim Novak? Who killed bloody Kim Novak? In fact, had her death been a bloody affair at all, or had she died peacefully in her sleep?

Edward glanced up from behind his computer as his line manager walked by. She wasn't interested in what he was or wasn't doing. He felt a twinge of guilt as he caught sight of a diligent colleague out of the corner of his eye; typing furiously. He had been like that: keen, eager, straight out of university with something to prove. No one here had been impressed, and with the lack of enthusiasm and encouragement, he'd lapsed quickly into apathy; only putting in an appearance for the money.

He wasn't even working now, instead just worrying about Kim Novak.

That morning he had received another anonymous note. Delivered in the usual fashion, this third one deviated from the standard; in fact, it was possible that a completely different recluse had sent it, although Edward was finding it hard enough to imagine that one person wanted to send him anonymous mail, let alone two. Whereas the first two had been print outs of newspaper articles and posters, this was just a handwritten message on an otherwise blank piece of paper. All the letters were capitals, and you could see that whoever had written it had inscribed each letter painstakingly slowly so that it would be impossible to see any kind of handwriting style from the note.

The question had been nagging ever since.

Who killed Kim Novak?

Naturally he had been straight onto the company Internet as soon as was respectable for a morning in the office. And his research had come up with the worst possible answer. Kim Novak wasn't even dead.

An old Hollywood film star, google had come up with links to several online biographies, all of which contained photographs that seemed vaguely familiar, although he couldn't place where from. He must have seen one of her films a long time ago. Born in the 1930s, still living today, Kim Novak was an American filmstar most noted for her role in the Hitchcock film *Vertigo*. No one had even made an assassination attempt on her life. There was nothing that could make any sense of the note – not that a note asking about the fate of an old film star was supposed to be logical. Even if she had been dead, it was still a strange message for someone to send to him.

He worried about it for the rest of the day. He sat and stared at the note on his way home on the bus, wondering if there was some cryptic, hidden message within the words. If there was, he wasn't seeing it.

On the way to the stairwell he bumped into Ray, who was heading out.

"Watch it, there," Ray warned, a little irritated by the close contact. "You got things on your mind?"

"Too much," Edward muttered, stalking into the building. He paused, looking back at Ray. "You ever had trouble with anonymous letters here?"

Ray smiled crookedly at him. "You got yourself a stalker, now?"

"Hardly." Edward sniffed at the idea. "Someone just keeps leaving me messages. Really weird ones."

"Weird how?"

"Well, look at this one." He passed Ray the now crumpled note. "See what I mean?"

Ray stood and studied the note for longer than what should have taken to read a sentence. "It is a weird one."

"Of course it is. I don't know why someone would want to ask me about Kim Novak. I looked her up on the Internet today."

"Kim?"

"Yes."

"Is she on the Internet?"

"Well, yes…" Edward faltered. Perhaps Ray hadn't heard of her before either. "And she's not even dead."

"Oh, she's dead all right. She drowned."

"What? No. I checked on wikipedia and the Internet movie database. She's definitely not dead."

Ray laughed as he handed back the note. "Oh, Jesus, yes, I was forgetting about that. Aye, Kim Novak the film star may well be still alive, right enough. I was thinking about Kim."

"Kim?"

"The woman who had your flat before."

Edward felt a little ill as he took back the note.

"I think her second name was Novak."

"And she drowned?"

"You don't need to look like that, it wasn't like she drowned in the bath or anything. I don't suppose you really needed to know the details, what with you living in her old flat, but there you go."

"Where did she drown?"

"In the Ouse."

The river in York. Edward's fingers tightened around the note. "So who killed her?"

"She killed herself. I remember she was a bit down beforehand. Depression and that." Ray paused, giving Edward's frightened countenance a disapproving look. "You needn't look like that. Jesus, someone's just messing with you. Ignore it."

Edward couldn't just ignore it. He was living in a dead woman's flat. A dead woman who had committed suicide. And someone was sending him anonymous notes about it. Perhaps it was Kim herself, from beyond the grave.

More disturbing than that was the fact that he had an inkling he knew where he had seen those Hollywood photos from before, and it wasn't from a film.

When he was back in his flat, he rooted through the papers, magazines and opened bills and bank statements that littered his bedroom floor until he found the two pieces of paper he wanted: the copy of the newspaper article and the missing persons poster. There she was, Judy Polwart, a twenty-four-year-old woman missing in York. Her body later recovered from the river Ouse. Her bleached white hair, high arching eyebrows of charcoal, her porcelain, innocent face that looked made for depression. And that striking resemble to Kim Novak.

Kim Novak, according to Ray, had lived in his flat before committing suicide. But it was Judy Polwart who had been in the papers. They couldn't possibly be the same person, could they?

The silence of living alone suddenly felt overwhelmingly penetrating. Edward glanced uncertainly around. Whatever had happened, whoever had actually lived here, why was someone sending him notes about something that had nothing to do with him? Asking who had killed a suicide victim.

He had only agreed to this because he had been curious. He was starting to resemble those cats and dogs you see in cartoons; caught by some brattish little girl who wants to play dollies and forces the kitty into the pram with a bib around its neck.

Sophia had looked at the bathroom mirror, the only mirror in his flat, and shook her head disapprovingly. It clearly was going to be hopeless here. She'd told him she had a couple of full length mirrors – for a moment Edward wondered if she meant on the ceiling – and didn't he think it was a good idea if they went up to her flat. Edward did think it was a good idea. He'd never been in Sophia's flat and was more than curious as to how the woman lived.

His suit had arrived from India, courtesy of the wonderful Mr Chin. Sophia was determined to show him just how right she was about tailoring, and said that they needed good mirrors if he were to appreciate the full effect. Edward had looked horrified as they'd unpacked the suit, realising that Mr Chin had included a matching waistcoat. Just how out of place did they want to make him feel?

Sophia fussed over him, giving him only the briefest of respites to actually change the basics over. Now he was fully dressed in Mr Chin's work, a little awkward and uncomfortable in the suit – so different to what he wore to work. Looking in the mirror and wondering who on earth he was gawking at. Edward felt unstylish but the man meeting his eye was incredibly well dressed, and the fact that he had a matching waistcoat didn't seem to matter. Thankfully the suit fabric was reasonably dark. If he'd have chosen a white or cream shade he would have probably looked like John Travolta getting down for some disco dancing. As it was, he didn't really recognise himself. But it did look very, very good.

"So you understand what I have been talking about?" Sophia asked, trotting across from the bathroom, still in her heels. It was easy to imagine her needing to get dressed up to do the dishes.

"Yes," Edward mumbled, still a little mesmerised by his new reflection. "I can't believe this is me."

"Tailoring does so much," Sophia confirmed. She had a pot of hair gel casually in her hand. "You've just got to be able to see the potential, and know how to bring it out." She paused, standing close by and examining the side of his head. She noted that his hair hadn't been cut for a while, and was getting quite long. As it was, it looked a bit scruffy, but this was early Friday evening just back from work. He'd probably scruffed himself up the moment he got in his flat, planning an undignified evening of slobbing in front of the television with beer and crisps.

The way she was examining him was getting uncomfortable. "Is everything all right?"

Sophia screwed off the lid of the hair gel. "I think you should do something with your hair as well," she said, taking a thick globule of hair gel out on the top of her scooped fingers. "If we give you a side parting like so, and slick your hair back and out to the side…"

Edward squirmed.

"I think that looks a lot better."

He met his eye in the mirror. His dark hair was right back off his forehead now, all sweeping across his scalp, an unnecessary comb over. His hair looked controlled to military standards. Sophia had really greased in the hair gel. He looked old fashioned, something almost timeless.

"I really think you should grow a moustache."

Edward snorted. "I'd look like a porn star."

"No you wouldn't. It would give you an air of distinction." Sophia said as she went to wash her hands.

Left alone in the living room, Edward took his eyes away from the mirror – he had to admit, the more he stared, the better looking he grew. He could quite fancy his chances looking like this in fact.

As much as he could have admired himself all day, whilst he had the chance, he really needed to get a better look around Sophia's home, if only to satisfy his own curiosity. Sophia's stamp was all over the flat the way some people start to resemble their dogs. It felt stylish, timeless and all very carefully thought out without looking as though she'd bought it all from a catalogue. As if it had all coincidentally tumbled together like this. And yet, it felt as though no one really lived here. It was tidy, really tidy, and there were hardly any knick knacks or personal mementoes littering the shelves. Perhaps she hadn't been living here very long.

Against one wall Sophia had two dark wood dressers, imposingly carved. The lower halves consisted of cupboards and drawers; the upper halves were bookshelves. Edward sauntered across, his new shoes squeaking. He cast an eye over the titles. There were a lot of large hardback coffee table books. Biographies. Glossy books full of photographs. In fact, there seemed to be quite a lot about film stars.

"Edward."

He jumped at the sound of his name. Her tone had sounded particularly angry, but when he turned around, she was stood, hands on hips and smiling.

"Why don't we go and see Archie?" she suggested. "Show him your new suit." She clapped her hands together as an idea occurred to her. "We can go out for drinks. You certainly don't need to feel uncomfortable anymore."

If Sophia had made him feel like a little boy, Archie finished the job off by slapping him on the back and commenting that people would mistake them for father and son. Edward hadn't thought Archie would be old enough to have a son his age, but then again, watching the man talk from the other side of the table when they were out at a bar, he decided that it was actually impossible to say exactly how old Archie really was. Maybe people would think they were related. Perhaps he should take Sophia's advice and grow a moustache; try to look a little older so no one would mistake him for a little boy playing at grown ups.

Mr Chin's spectacular creation attracted a lot of attention over the coming weeks. As Edward wore it day by day, his body and the cut of the suit settling against one another, he gradually ceased to feel out of place. He grew into the style, and felt the better for it.

People looked at him in a different way at work. The first morning he had walked into the office, fully suited complete with waistcoat, hair carefully in place, a hush fell upon workstations near his own desk. His line manager had even sounded pleasant towards him. People treated him in a different way, seeing him as someone who now commanded respect. A grown up. But not just an adult, someone special. Someone you didn't want to miss an opportunity with.

A couple of weeks after the event, the Gable family gathered in Durham to celebrate his mother's birthday. He'd arrived in the front hall, set his rucksack down by the staircase. His father had stepped out of the living room and raised his eyebrows when he saw the change in his son.

"Blimey," he exclaimed, surprised that one of his offspring could scrub up quite so well: smartly dressed and, dare he say it, dashing. "What's happened to you?"

Edward shrugged as it if were nothing. "Just got a new suit." Soon to be joined by two others. Edward was converted.

"York's agreeing with you, then?"

"Oh yes."

"Jean, love, you have to have a look at this. Our Edward's turned into Mr Sophistication."

His mother's face appeared around the door. "Goodness, Edward. You do look smart. Is this for my birthday celebrations?"

"Of course. A little belated, but we get there in the end."

"James is supposed to be landing in the next hour," she told him. "He's driving over."

His father loitered in the doorway as Edward and his mother sat down on the settee. "I'm a little intrigued by this change, I must say. Would I be right in guessing there's a woman involved?"

His father made it sound like a joke. Taking a step back towards childhood. "Not in the way you mean. Sophia's just been helping me a bit."

"Sophia, eh?" He smiled knowingly and nodded at Jean.

Edward decided to ignore their knowing looks and focused on the television. His mother was part way through watching a film. It looked as though it was set on a small tropical island. It was one of those things that if you came to it, half way through, it really did beggar comprehension. A dishevelled man was trying to make repairs on a small boat that was beached in a small lagoon, except small, scruffily dressed girls continued to run around and annoy him. The man looked weary and irritated by it all, with a loose shirt that probably hadn't seen an iron in years, and several days worth of stubble on his face.

Jean peered closely at her son. He didn't look like he'd shaved in a couple of days, which was a regular occurrence for Edward, and being dark haired, it showed quickly, yet there was something more planned behind all this. "Are you growing a moustache?"

He felt uncomfortable. His confidence was faltering. "I was thinking about it."

An interfering dark-haired woman had come into the scene.

"Felt like a bit of a change?"

"Yeah."

"Sophia thought it was a good idea?"

Edward leaned forward and focused on the film, trying to ignore his father. The grumpy man in the film looked like he wanted a drink. It was strange, but if you gave him a shave and a suit, he started to resemble someone he knew. "That guy there," he started, looking over at his mother. "He looks like one of my neighbours."

"Really," his mother sounded only marginally interested.

"Yeah. His name is Archie." Edward settled back into the settee. "He's a really friendly guy. Gave me a bottle of bourbon to welcome me to the building. Always enthusiastic about everything. Bit weird in a way." He mused over the few occasions he had had contact with Archie. "Got a bit of a weird name as well. Leach. Doesn't really suit him."

"Archie Leach," his mother sighed, repeating the name without really listening. She was lost in her film.

"Archie Leach?" his father said, quite obviously paying close attention. He watched a few seconds of the film then burst into laughter. "What, Archibald Leach?"

Edward didn't see what was funny. "I suppose it's short for Archibald."

"I think someone's having you on." His father pointed at the television. "Archie Leach lives next door to Edward. You'd never have guessed, would you?"

Jean smiled weakly, getting the joke but wishing her husband would either shut up or go away and let her get on with watching her film.

Edward looked bewildered. He didn't understand. "I don't get what's so funny."

"Happy Birthday!"

The front door crashed open, and Edward's elder brother, James stormed into the house. "I have returned home," he announced, coming into the living room. "Mother, you're not watching films again? Quit the reminiscing and let's get going. We've got a table booked, haven't we? I'm sorry I'm a bit late, but I'm not that late." He broke off, looking Edward up and down. "Bloody hell, you're smartly dressed. We're not going that up market are we?" he added, glancing down at his best jeans and smart T-shirt (the one with absolutely no swearing on it) and wondering if he was going to be underdressed.

"Oh no," their mother assured them, abruptly stopping the film and switching the television off. "Edward just felt like a change, and he looks very nice, so you two can let him alone. There's nothing wrong with wanting to make a bit of an effort now and then."

He got a text message from Toby in the middle of the week suggesting that they should meet up. He hadn't seen Toby for weeks; they hadn't really socialised for months, in fact the last time Edward could remember seeing Toby had been at the showdown with Sophia just after Mr Chin had measured him for a suit. Despite the lack of contact, not really knowing what Toby was up to at the moment, he felt as though he was growing away from his old friends and life. He replied anyway and suggested they meet up straight after work.

They met in the centre of town. Toby almost walked past Edward at first, then slowed and took a step backwards. "Jesus, man," he exclaimed, giving Edward a curious stare. "What's with the moustache? Are you trying to look like some dodgy porn star?"

"I don't look like a porn star."

"Yeah, whatever," Toby looked his old university mate up and down. "That's a fancy suit."

"Proper tailoring."

Toby snorted. "I think you've been spending too much time with that snooty bitch."

How would you know, we've barely seen each other the last few weeks, Edward thought to himself, but didn't say it out loud. Toby would have just called him an old woman and accused him of being jealous.

Toby then proceeded to surprise Edward not once but twice.

"I can't be arsed going to the pub."

"What?"

"Shall we just go back to yours and order pizza?"

Edward's eyebrows went up even higher.

"Or have you turned your flat into a porn nest?"

Toby really was an arsehole at times. "I don't think you've ever been up my way."

Toby snorted.

They went to the bus stop, placing themselves at the end of a long queue of bored looking workers wanting to go home. Toby slouched against the long black iron railings that lined in front of the imposing council buildings. He looked as though he could think of at least ten places he would rather be. It was incomprehensible why he'd decided to meet up with Edward.

"So, anything exciting been happening at your block of flats?"

Edward looked suspiciously at his friend. There was an ulterior motive to this meeting. Obviously it had something to do with where he lived, and he doubted it was because Toby wanted to enjoy the pleasure of his company. "Not much. I keep getting anonymous letters though."

"Really?" Toby perked up a little. "Have you got a stalker or something?"

"Not exactly. Someone just keeps leaving me articles and things about this woman who drowned herself."

"Death threats."

Edward gave him a look. "She lived in the flat before I moved in."

"Do you think it was murder?"

"I think it was suicide."

"Like you'd know. We could ask her."

"Who?" He looked up the street where the road took a sharp turn to the right, heading up over the river and towards the railway station. The girl was walking towards them. She smiled self-consciously at Edward and pretended Toby wasn't there.

"You live with Edward, don't you?" Toby blurted out, neglecting to consider they'd never really been introduced. He remembered seeing her in passing once and that was enough for him to accost her.

She looked a little startled. "We live on the same floor."

"Do you know about the dead woman who lived in Ed's flat?"

She was paler than usual; her eyes rounder and more afraid. Her big deer eyes, caught in headlights. "I forgot something."

"What?" Toby leered forward. He didn't understand people who lacked in confidence.

"In town." She turned and headed back down the road towards the city centre.

"What the hell was that about?" Toby turned on Edward. "You live in a block full of freaks, do you know that? Dead women and Italian snobs and that…" he paused and watched her, walking over the road in the crowds as the pedestrian crossing flashed green. "What is her name, anyway?"

"I don't know," Edward said wistfully, watching her hurry down the pedestrian street straight ahead.

"You don't know? Don't you have much to do with her?"

"I see her quite a bit."

"And you don't know what she's called?"

"The longer it is, the harder it is to ask."

Toby laughed as their bus appeared around the corner. "She's weird anyway, I don't think it's worth chasing her name."

When they got off the bus and walked up to Edward's building, Toby started to get restless. His mood grew increasingly worse as they entered at the ground floor. He pointed at Lexie's door. "Has she moved out?"

Edward glanced at the direction of Toby's finger. "No, she's still here. She's just taken down the name sign."

"And she's the cat's mother."

Lexie had appeared in the doorway behind them. Lit up from behind by the exterior light, sunlight coming through her fluffed up blonde hair, she looked almost angelic, if it weren't for the coy look in her eye. She'd painted her lips a particular shade of red that just screamed sex. Her eyelashes looked so long that they were weighting her eyelids down.

Toby stood and gawped.

Lexie walked across to her flat, looking down at Toby. "Evening."

The voice was familiar but the appearance wasn't at all how he remembered. "Lexie?" Toby sounded uncertain of himself.

"Oh yes, that's me. Except these days they're calling me Marilyn."

"I can see why."

Lexie unlocked her flat door and stepped inside. "I'll be seeing you around."

Toby started forward. "We should catch up."

"We should, but we won't." She shut the door in his face.

Edward turned and smiled a wide smile of satisfaction. Nothing less was deserved.

PART THREE

James was trying to look through the spy hole the wrong way round. His face wore a strange expression as if he was in discomfort. His pained look appeared all the more excruciating from the tunnel effect of the spy glass. Edward couldn't remember ever seeing his brother looking quite this way before.

It was Friday night and normal people were either out on the town or slobbed out in front of the television, exhausted by a week of work. James hadn't said he was coming down to York for the weekend; he'd just appeared. Looking a bit odd. Something was definitely amiss.

He jumped back as Edward opened the door. "Edward!" he cried out, a little too gleefully as if he had something to hide. He glanced his brother's suit up and down. "You going out?"

"No. What are you doing here?"

"I've come to visit you." James waggled a rucksack at him as if that much should have been obvious. "I haven't even seen your new flat yet. Mind if I come in?"

"I suppose not." Edward stood and watched as James strode into the small flat, glancing here and there as if checking for emergency exits. "You could have told me you were coming."

"Why, got plans?" James lurched back into the corridor, having made his brief inspection of the bathroom. "You seeing this woman of yours?"

Edward rolled his eyes and stalked into the living room. The television was still on, from where he had been before the knock at the door. He had muted the sound when he had got up to answer the door. The glare from the screen cast out a hollow light. James flicked on the main light.

"You've been sent down by Mum, haven't you?"

"Mum *and* Dad, actually," James said matter of factly, sitting down in the armchair. "They are a bit worried about you. About you living alone here."

"Just because I got a suit."

"I think it was the moustache that really threw them off balance." He scrutinised his brother. "Are you growing side burns now?"

Edward glared at him.

He sighed, and leant back into the seat. "You don't need to get so defensive, they're just worried about you. You can see why, really, you suddenly dressing differently, getting a moustache like a porn star."

"I am not a porn star."

"I really hope things haven't gotten that bad."

Edward fought back a little smile.

"They're just worried that some woman's having a little bit more influence over you than what might be strictly healthy. What with all the appearance changes and that. You have just started living all on your lonesome for the first time. I think they're worried you've joined a cult or something."

Edward snorted. "I'm not called James."

"That was not a cult."

"Look, I've not got some nutter girlfriend," Edward offered a ceasefire, dropping on to the settee. "I haven't got a girlfriend of any description. I just got a bit of advice about some clothes, that's all. I just wanted to look smart."

"Nothing wrong with that."

They both looked down at James' torn jeans.

"Well, if that's all settled, I think we need to bring some alcohol in on the situation," James decided, drawing attention away from his less than attractive trainers by setting his rucksack in front of his feet. "I've got a couple of great alien DVDs as well," he added, unzipping the bag.

"I've got some beer in the fridge." Edward got up to go to the kitchen.

There was a clatter as James tossed some DVDs in the direction of the television. "Sorry if I pissed you off back there, but Mum was worried about you and bugged me into coming down to visit and check up on you. You know what she can be like sometimes. Besides, she probably got the wrong end of the stick." James laughed to himself, thinking over the telephone conversation.

Edward passed him a beer. "Surely they should be worried if I'm on drugs or something, not because I grew a moustache."

"Yeah. It's just Mum," James shook his head to himself. "She's got it into her head that you think you're living with Cary Grant."

Edward laughed. "Yeah, right. Old dead filmstars." He'd heard of the name but didn't know that much more about the actor.

"Mum was watching *Father Goose* the other weekend. She said that you'd said your neighbour looked just like Cary Grant."

Edward remembered the film. The grumpy man in his scruffy shirt, looking in desperate need of a shave, with little school children running around irritating the hell out of him. "That was Cary Grant? Well, yes, one of my neighbours does look like him."

"Well, that happens." James shrugged, opening his can. "Just as long as you don't think he really is Cary Grant."

"I have no delusions about the man. His name is Archie."

James stared steadily at his brother.

Edward felt a little uncomfortable. "Archie Leach."

"Archibald Leach?" James sounded unimpressed.

"Yes. I know it's a bit of a weird…"

"Are you a complete cretin?" James thumped his can on the floor, liquid spilling up into the rim.

"No!"

"Archibald Leach was Cary Grant. Cary Grant was just a stage name. Maybe there really is something wrong with you."

"There's nothing wrong with me." Edward stood up. "Come down and look at the list of names. You come and see that Archie is his name."

"All right then," James didn't sound like he believed him. "You show me."

On the ground floor, near to the entrance, there was a list of flats with occupants' names laid out like a building plan. Really for the postman and deliveries, Edward supposed, but it would certainly prove to James that he wasn't going mad.

"There." He tapped the top line. "Archibald Leach. I am not making it up."

James peered closely at the board. "You're not joking, are you. That's bloody weird, if he really does look like Cary Grant as well." He paused, looking at the name next to Archie's, marking the flat next door. "There's an S Loren living here."

"That's Sophia."

James snorted incredulously.

"What's your problem?"

"You live next door to Cary Grant *and* Sophia Loren?"

Edward didn't know quite how to respond to that one. He hadn't really thought about people's names all that much. Now that James pointed it out, now that he mocked the coincidence, Edward was starting to feel a bit ill.

James didn't seem to notice the look of sinking horror on his brother's face. "And who lives on the next floor? Margaret Hayworth."

"Everyone calls her Rita."

"What else?" James commented drolly. "And what about this Welles here? Who lives across from Rita? Or let me guess, it's Orson, right?"

"Yes." Edward said, his voice strained.

James' finger traced down the board, past the scrubbed out entry where the girl's name ought to have been, past his own entry: Edward Gable, and down to the ground floor.

"Well, these two seem to be normal. Alexandra Monroe and Ray O'Donnell."

"Ray used to work as a Humphrey Bogart impersonator."

James turned to him, his eyebrows raised.

"And Lexie recently changed her name by deed poll to Marilyn."

"If it wasn't for the look on your face, I'd think this was a piss take. You seriously never noticed any of this? This is a really weird place you're living."

"Not as weird as the anonymous letters I've been getting."

"Please tell me you're joking."

He shook his head. "Come on, I'll show you."

The two brothers sat the kitchen table; the notes laid out before them.

"I got this one first," Edward explained, pointing to the photocopy of a newspaper page. "And then the poster. About this girl, Judy, who went missing. She drowned in the river."

"She looks a bit like Kim Novak."

"And Ray told me that the woman who lived in this flat before me was called Kim. She committed suicide. She drowned."

James looked worried. "I think you need to find somewhere new to live."

"But the rent's really cheap here."

"There's obviously a reason for that."

"I can't afford a flat on my own. I like living here."

"It's just all so bloody weird." James put his hand to his mouth thoughtfully. "And I can't even see any point to it. Or how you'd do it, or why, or anything. I think you need to find out why you're getting these anonymous notes."

"And before I do that, I need to find out who's sending them." Edward collected up the letters and put them back in the kitchen drawer.

James shook his head again in disbelief. "This would be funny if it wasn't for that woman's death."

Rita opened the door, unintentionally seductive towards any caller. Leaning on the edge of the door, a hand draped down the side, she smiled in amusement at James, who in turn stared agog straight back at her.

"Well, Edward, who's your friend?"

He didn't know what it was about Rita, but she always managed to make him feel unsophisticated; in a completely unmalicious way of course, but never the less, Edward felt as though one of them had been time travelling. Perhaps if he'd come in his suit, he would have felt better, but James had bullied him into putting jeans and a T-shirt on.

Rita looked like she was off to a boating regatta; navy, high-waisted, cropped trousers, a white, large collared shirt tied at the waist and a red scarf around her neck. Her hair was loose but worryingly styled for a Saturday morning, set in perfect waves to her shoulders.

"This is my brother, James," Edward blurted out.

"Really?" She held out a hand to James. "Nice to meet you."

James looked as though he was meeting a real celebrity. Edward glared at his brother – so much for trying to be intellectually superior on this one.

"You busy at the moment?"

"I was just about to start a book," Rita said. There was no response to her answer; the two brothers remaining on her doorstep like dummies. Her ruby lips curled in amusement. "Well, Edward, would you and your brother like to come in for some tea?"

"Would we?" James burst out, speaking for the first time. He shoved past Edward and followed Rita eagerly into her flat.

A little disgruntled, Edward took up the rear, closing the door behind him.

Rita's flat seemed to radiate inner peace. The corridor was painted a clean, fresh white, with Chinese paintings hung on strips of silk. James followed Rita into the kitchen whilst she made the tea. Edward hung out in the doorway, looking at a stylised painting of juniper trees on a misty mountain top. He watched through the doorway as Rita took a Chinese tea set down from a shelf and started to make green tea.

James had wandered across to the kitchen table, above which a large red Chinese lantern was hanging. "You ever been to Shanghai, Rita?"

"I haven't, actually," she answered, concentrating on pouring the boiling water into the little teapot. "Although my father comes from Beijing."

"So you're not the lady from Shanghai?"

Edward caught James' eye, scowling at him and mouthing the question 'what the hell?' Rita just laughed lightly, understanding more than Edward. "No, I'm afraid not." She picked up the tray and turned to the doorway. "Shall we go through to the living room?"

The living room was like something out of a 1920s film of colonial Britain in the tropics. A massive wooden fan hung from the middle of the ceiling, stationary at present, but Edward couldn't imagine her ever having much call for it in this country. The walls were painted caramel; large leafy plants – palms, bamboo, rubber plants and lemon and orange trees in large brass plant pots clustered in the corners. All the furniture involved caning: cane chairs with cream cushions, a cane coffee table with a glass top. The brothers took an armchair each. Rita set the tray on the table, pouring out three cups of tea before retreating to the cushioned window seat. She opened the window behind her wide before turning to the two brothers.

"Well, Edward, I think this must be the first time you've been in here since you helped with my desk. And now I get to meet your brother."

Edward smiled awkwardly as he picked up his ceramic beaker of tea. It did seem a bit ridiculous and forward that they'd come to pay her a call. "James is up for the weekend."

"So I see." Rita lent forward and pulled an inlayed wooden box on the coffee table towards her.

"Are you aware of what you are?" James asked.

Edward coughed into his tea in horror.

Rita held her perfect composure. She merely looked questioningly at James, not bothering to answer or ask what he meant. She flicked back the lid of the box. "Do either of you boys smoke?"

Edward shook his head, James ignored the question. "I mean, you're not going to try and tell us all of this is coincidental and unplanned," James persisted. "You can't have just happened upon this way of dressing for yourself and be called Rita Hayworth."

Rita took a cigarette from the box. "Officially, I'm called Margaret."

"But everyone calls you Rita. Everyone but your Scottish mother."

Rita set the cigarette between her lips, lit it and inhaled deeply before lazily hanging her arm, cigarette caught between two fingers, out of the window. She blew out a curl of smoke like a dragon's tail. "I hope you don't mind if I smoke. We're not supposed to smoke in these flats, but it is my home, and as long as I keep the window open, I really don't see the problem."

James was like a dog with a bone. "You don't think you're Rita Hayworth?"

"I am Rita Hayworth," she told him, a hint of sharpness creeping into her voice. She lifted up her arm and took another drag on the cigarette. The epitome of cool, but Edward noticed that her hand was shaking slightly. "I get the impression you're confusing me with someone else," she said pointedly at James. "I don't believe people come back from the dead, and despite my roots, I don't believe in reincarnation either."

"But you're called what you're called and you dress how you dress."

"I wasn't aware it was a copyrighted name and look." Rita flicked some ash outside. "You know, I had been planning on relaxing this morning, reading a book. I hadn't been planning on being harassed."

James sank back into the armchair. "Look, I didn't ask my brother to bring me up here so I could pick a fight with you."

"You didn't?" She sounded as though she was mocking him.

"The family's just worried about Edward. He's been acting a bit funny recently. I came down to see him this weekend and he's been telling me about the people living here."

Rita pursed her lips. "I'm sure no one's been threatening him."

"No, but you're all named after old Hollywood film stars."

She just shrugged. "Truth is stranger than fiction."

James was getting irritated by her complacency. "You can't tell me you don't find that just a little bit weird. This is not normal. Is there something in the water supply that's making you all deluded?"

"We're not deluded," she started, before pausing thoughtfully. "Well, I'm certainly not. But I don't know why you're all worried about Edward. He looks perfectly fine to me. It seems a little patronising that you think he's got problems."

"He has though," James retorted, not willing to admit she probably had a point; desperately groping for something more he could use. "He's been getting anonymous letters."

Rita's brow knitted, for the first time looking concerned by anything James had to say. "Really?" She lent forward and stubbed out her cigarette in a clean, glass ashtray. "What kind of letters?"

"They've not been threatening," Edward quickly said before James could start up on another tirade. "They've just been a bit weird. About the woman who lived in my flat before me. Well, I think they are. Ray told me her name was Kim, but two of these are about a woman called Judy." He took the folded letters out of his back pocket and passed them to Rita.

Carefully unfolding the papers, Rita read them, sitting in silence for a few minutes before slowly nodding. "They are all about the same person. But I don't see why you need to know." She glanced up at him. "It's not upsetting you to know that she's dead now?"

Edward shook his head. "I never knew her."

"So who was she?" James asked. "Judy or Kim."

Rita sighed, setting the letters on the coffee table. Draping herself glamorously in the window seat, she looked from one brother to the other. "She was Judy when she moved in. I think she'd suffered from depression in the past. She probably shouldn't have been living on her own."

"So who's Kim?"

"She changed her name."

"To Kim Novak. Like Lexie did?"

"Lexie's changed her name to Kim Novak?" Rita looked up sharply.

Edward shook his head. "Marilyn."

"Marilyn?" She didn't immediately understand the choice of name. "Oh, of course, she's a Monroe."

James was a little baffled by her complacency towards all of what he viewed as madness. Even the news regarding Edward's anonymous letters didn't seem to bother her all that much. Or if these things concerned her, she was keeping it all very low below the surface.

"I really don't get why you're all pretending to be film stars..."

"No one's pretending," Rita said.

"I mean," James continued, "Did it all just start as a bit of a laugh and it got out of hand? Did you go to a fancy dress party and decide the party should never end?"

Rita was looking increasingly irritated. "I don't know why you think I should know; I haven't been living here all that long."

"So this was all going when you moved in? Is that why you moved in or did you just get caught up in it?"

Rita ignored James' questions.

"Who's been living here the longest?"

She looked directly at Edward, James no longer existing for her. "I don't know why you're expecting me to have all the answers. You need to speak to someone who's been living here a long time. Archie or Sophia. But I'd think carefully before I started digging too much, if I were you."

The conspiracy – that was what James was calling it now – was functioning on different levels, and there were two things that Edward needed to find out. Strange how it was now Edward who had to solve everything on his own, now that James had run out of ideas. Edward didn't even see the thing as a matter of urgency; although having listened to James' outside opinion all weekend had unsettled him a little.

He had seen his brother off at the station. James reminded him that he needed to dig up the background – why this odd tradition of mimicry had started – the hows, whys and wherefores; and find out who was responsible. Edward didn't see that it was really any of his business, but James was too busy listing off orders to take note of little brother's concerns.

So what if a few people had odd names; it was hardly illegal and they weren't hurting anyone. Or at least most of them had names. Edward sat in the kitchen and stared out of the window to the road below.

That brought them to the other problem. Who was sending these anonymous letters and why? The act of anonymity denoted a fear of being found out. Found out of what, he wasn't sure exactly, but he had seen that kind of fear here before. And he knew a girl without a name.

He watched her get off the bus and walk up to the building. A few moments, then he could hear her footsteps as she ascended the staircase. She'd pause, take her keys out of her coat pocket and unlock the flat door. He really ought to confront her. They'd known each other too long to be playing silly games like this. Besides which, at this stage in a friendship, it was only polite that he knew her name.

It took Edward a while to find the courage to go over to her flat. He wasn't naturally inclined for confrontation. Sometimes we have to do these things, he told himself as he waited for her to answer the door.

The girl smiled when she saw it was him, and let him into the flat. "Edward!" she greeted him. "Lovely to see you. Are you having a nice weekend?"

She was a lot more relaxed and cheery than he usually found her. She led him into the living room and returned to where she had been sitting. There was a wide arc of photographs spread over the carpet. She placed herself on the floor in the centre like an imp.

"I got some photos developed," she told him, her eyes dropping down to the pictures. "It may look as though I've taken the entire lab back home with me, but I haven't, honest."

Edward smiled awkwardly and perched on the arm of the settee, feeling uncomfortable. "My brother was over visiting for the weekend."

"Oh really. Was it his first time in York?"

"No."

"Oh," her voice faltered, feeling the tension.

"He was a bit worried about me, and to be honest, I'm a bit worried now. I've been getting these anonymous letters through the door."

"Anonymous letters?" her brow crinkled, not having expected him to come out with something like that. "Do you mean threatening letters?"

Playing it cool, very good. He was impressed, but then she wasn't as fragile and naïve as she put across – she had very naturally managed never to let him find out some of the most basic information about her during these last months.

"No. Just letters about this woman called Judy. Although I think everyone knew her as Kim."

She was looking uncertain again. That frightened animal look.

"Kim Novak."

"Kim Novak," she repeated slowly.

"Come on, you can't tell me you don't know what I'm talking about, considering she lived across the landing from you. She lived in my flat. Until she topped herself."

She wrung her hands together. "I know who she was," she spoke softly.

"Well, now that's all in the open, I don't see why you don't just come out and tell me what these letters mean."

"Sorry?"

"I know it was you!" Edward accused her, growing exasperated with her good-natured innocence. "You're the only person who could have been sending those letters. You might as well just say what you've got to say."

"But I've got nothing to say."

"There must be something. There's got to be a reason. Anonymous letters mean someone's afraid of something. You're the only one around here who looks like that."

"I did not send those notes."

"Yes you did. You're always scuttling about, avoiding people. For crying out loud, I don't even know what you're called." There, he'd said it. In any other friendship, such an admission at this point would have been a poor move, bringing forward offence and incense. She seemed to accept this; of course she would. She made sure he didn't know who she was. "I don't know who you are."

"Of course you know me. We've spend a lot of time together."

"I don't know what you're called."

She avoided his eye. "You've no right to accuse me of sending you letters. Besides, surely you ought to be clever enough to figure out what they mean, especially if you've had more than one. You who's on the graduate training scheme."

The sharpness stung, although not quite as much as the fact it was coming from her lips. In a way, it was just defensive, but Edward was too blinkered to see anyone but himself as the victim in all of this right now. "Well, what's your name then? Or are you too secretive to even admit to having a name? Do you think you're so above the rest of us that I don't deserve to know?"

A courage he hadn't seen in her before appeared in her eyes. She was steady, controlled, but on the edge of breaking up into uncontrollable shaking. She looked coldly up at him. "It should take you about six seconds to get from here to the door," she spoke, sitting up straight, regal and icy. "I'll give you three."

Edward stormed out, slamming the door behind him. Back in his own flat, he threw a couple of ugly teacups at the wall. Ugly teacups his mother had insisted on leaving in his new first home. He went back to the kitchen window to sulk. He had learned absolutely nothing - not even her name - from that confrontation; the only thing he could say was that he'd really ticked off the closest friend he had in this whole nuthouse. He could be really stupid sometimes.

Sophia had answered the door in white suede boots that went up past her knees. The hem of her white sleeveless dress just brushed the top of the boots, making them almost look like impracticable biking trousers.

It was raining outside. The mist had built up in the vale – the long valley-like section between the Moors and the Dales, at the base of which sat York. They hadn't seen the sun for days. Pressed down under layers of cloud. Edward hadn't seen the girl since their argument, and it wasn't the kind of thing he knew how to come back from, so he avoided being out in the stairwell too long. He'd worried he'd see her at the bus stop when going to work, but she never appeared. As if she'd never even existed in the first place.

He'd tried calling on Sophia a few times, but this was the first time she'd been home. It was Sophia and Archie he'd really wanted to talk to, as the longest serving residents. As if they knew this, they had left. The upper floor of the building silent for days. Sophia was quick to explain why, without even needing to be asked.

"I was in Milan with Archie," she said, giving a little kick of her boots as she led him back into the flat. The boots had come from Milan. Perhaps even a gift from Archie. "We had the most wonderful time. We got back yesterday. Was such a shame to come home. And look at it out there."

Edward didn't need to look out of the window to know it was still raining. He watched Sophia go back to the full-length mirror in the living room, brushing her hair. She was positively glowing. Must have been a good trip. He had suspected there was a thing going on between Sophia and Archie, and he supposed this confirmed it. Although he couldn't imagine Archie permanently settling down with anyone, somehow. He seemed too much a confirmed bachelor.

The carnage of Sophia's holiday was still scattered over the room. A pull along suitcase was slumped tiredly on the settee, its top zipped right back to reveal an untidy scattering of clothes. There was lots of tissue paper spilling out of a long cardboard box that would have probably once contained the boots. A couple of Italian paperbacks and a crumpled newspaper, also in Italian, were on top of a chest of drawers, along with a couple of bottles of spirits and a nest of tickets and a passport.

Sophia waved a hand at the bottles. "Archie's left some things here still. Some of his duty free. I didn't want to buy any alcohol, so he used my allowance."

"Oh."

She was now twisting the length of her hair around one hand before beginning to pin it up on the back of her head.

"Are you going out somewhere?"

"I'm going to meet some friends in town," she said, concentrating on her reflection as she pinned up her hair. "But not for an hour, don't worry. What did you want?"

"You and Archie have been living here the longest, haven't you?"

"Well, Archie was here before I moved in. But yes, I am second veteran after Archie." Sophia's laughter tinkled.

"I was wondering about the woman who lived in my flat."

"Why, Edward!" Sophia exclaimed in amusement. "You do ask the most strange questions. Why do you need to worry about the people who lived there before you?"

"Some people have told me that she died." He didn't mention the anonymous letters. He'd seen the animosity that Sophia had regarded the girl with. Whilst they were no longer on speaking terms, he still didn't feel he could betray her to Sophia.

Sophia's smile dropped a fraction. "People die sometimes," she responded. "You know that. None of us is designed to live forever. Now, who has been trying to frighten you?"

She looked into the mirror and her reflected gaze penetrated Edward. She had stopped fussing with her hair; giving him her full attention. Edward felt that no one would thank him for mentioning their names to Sophia. "No one in particular," he replied.

There was a touch of doubt on her face, but she looked as though she didn't want to pursue it.

"But I'd really like to know how long the building has been like this."

"Been like this?" Sophia asked as she put her earrings in. "I'm afraid I'm not an expert of architecture."

"I didn't mean the architecture. I mean the people living here. When did you all decide to pretend to be the Hollywood walk of fame?"

Her brow creased in consternation. "What do you mean? No one is pretending to be anything."

"But what about the way you all dress? You really stand out from the crowd."

Sophia broke into a sympathetic smile. "Oh Edward," she sighed, turning around to face him properly. "We're back to tailoring again, aren't we? Good cut, great quality, timeless style. Of course we all look good against the crowd. Most people have no idea of what looks good on them normally." She walked around behind him so that they were both staring into the mirror. "Look at you; you're just the same as we are, dressed in your suit. You look classically stylish. I can imagine your work colleagues really look up to you now."

Edward regarded himself self-consciously.

"I see you took my advice about the moustache as well," Sophia continued. "It looks really good. Now, I must find my handbag."

She left him mesmerised by his reflection, the heels on her boots tapping against the wood flooring as she wandered through to her bedroom looking for her bag.

This wasn't enough. Edward tore his eyes away from the mirror. "But what about the names?" he called out to her. "You can't say everyone's names are just tailoring. And it's not just a funny coincidence. It's just bloody weird."

"There's nothing weird about anyone's name that I can see. People are called what they are because that's their name. It's nothing to do with me."

He didn't feel like he was going to get a straight answer. Wandering over to the sideboard, he picked up one of the bottles; a square shaped bottle full of a dark brown liquid. Amaretti. A sharp rich scent of marzipan. He suspected it was Archie's. Why had Archie left his things over here? Edward's eyes scanned across the top; tickets from Milan airport; a receipt in Italian. There was a passport lying face down. He picked it up and turned it over, seeing it was a British passport. Why would Archie leave such an important document with Sophia?

Edward looked furtively up. Sophia was still in the other room. He could hear her moving about. He glanced back down at the passport, and flicked it open to the back, wanting to know if Archie was really, honestly truly and legally called Archibald Leach.

But it wasn't Archie's face that looked back at him. Sophia's carefully made up face stared coolly up from the page. Sophia Loren. She had told him that she was Italian. She even spoke with an accent. Edward read over the information. She had been born in the seventies. She was thirty-three now. She had been born in Leeds.

"Edward?"

He jumped, panicking, and quickly replaced the passport as Sophia returned to the room. She hadn't seen that he had been looking.

"Why are you so worried about everyone's names? Do you feel that you don't fit in?"

Edward didn't feel very well anymore. "I don't know," he mumbled, backing for the door. "I'd better let you get on, Sophia. You don't want to be late for your friends."

The weeks drifted by in something of a haze. He didn't see the girl, not even in passing in the stairwell, although he could feel the disapproval coming from her flat. He became reclusive: went to work, came straight back home, stayed in the flat. Lexie came by a couple of times. Except she wasn't calling herself Lexie anymore. The first time he noticed she'd changed her name badge for work to

Marilyn; the second time, when he asked through the door who was there, she'd replied in her broad Glaswegian accent, 'Marilyn'. Now that she was stuck with it, she might as well use it, she'd reasoned.

He'd ordered another suit from Mr Chin, which had arrived promptly. Edward's new style was establishing itself, and although small, his wardrobe had taken on a whole new look. People at work continued to treat him with distinct respect, as if with the suit he had bought in a new maturity and intelligence. And yet underneath the good tailoring, he was still exactly the same person – reminded of the fact every time someone opened their mouth and said: "Edward?"

He didn't get anymore anonymous letters. Presumably the showdown with the girl had put her off trying to frighten him. If that was what her ultimate aim had been. Now that her anonymity was blown, she wouldn't want to continue. Kim Novak drifted to the back of his mind; the letters were swallowed up in the mess of old newspapers and bank statements drifting down beside the settee.

Edward spent a lot of his free time sitting in the flat wondering who he was.

He woke his brother up at three in the morning on a work night. He had rung the mobile number three times before James had picked up and answered rather than leaving it to go to voicemail.

"Edward, what the fuck do you think you're doing?" he barked into the phone. "It is three o'clock in the bloody morning."

"I got some paperwork in the post today."

He could hear his brother sigh in exasperation. He would want to hang up, tell his brother to stick his paperwork where the sun didn't shine, especially at this time of night. But promises to mother dearest to look after his younger sibling would pray on his conscience. Edward never did things like this. The old Edward didn't anyway.

"You got something in the post today, that's great." James sounded as if he was trying to talk a lunatic away from the edge of a building. "It wasn't an anonymous note, was it?"

"No, that's stopped."

"Great." Silence. James wasn't a natural born counsellor. "So what's going on? Are you having a nervous breakdown or something, Edward? Because normal people don't ring up other normal people to tell them they got post at three o'clock in the morning."

"I've done something really stupid," Edward started. His voice sounded weak, as if it were about to break up. "Mum's going to kill me."

"Mum? What have you done? Where's this post come from?"

"Deed poll."

There was silence on the phone. "You've changed your name?" James finally coughed. "What the hell were you thinking? Shit. So you're not one of the Gable boys anymore? Dad's going to be really unimpressed."

"I'm still a Gable."

Uncertain silence with a crackle in the connection replied. It was all slipping into place. James was feeling foolish for not having seen this sooner. "So there was a reason for you growing that moustache."

"I didn't realise at the time."

"And quite frankly, you couldn't give a damn now," James quipped. "Shit. Look, something's got to be done. You can't keep living there and letting this happen. Don't speak to anyone else about this until I've figured out what to do. Understood?"

"Understood."

Orson was parking his car as Edward was walking back home from the bus stop. Edward's eyes were heavily bagged – he was barely sleeping these days. It was making him look older, wearier of life. He bore a heavy weight on his back: in the rucksack lay the letter from deed poll thanking him for his application to change his name. Please fill in and sign the enclosed forms and you can begin the process to become Clark Gable.

He didn't know what to do with the letter. He couldn't let it out of his sight, because he knew what had happened to Marilyn, previously known as

Lexie. But there was something holding him back that stopped him from tearing it all to shreds, setting it alight and reclaiming his own identity. Something perverse that said it would be fun to do. You only live once. He felt as though he was going mad.

One of the girls at work had asked him out today. A girl had asked *him*. Said she'd never noticed before how masculine he was. He'd got a style and an aura that other guys of their generation simply lacked. He stood out. He was wanted. Edward had never been overly successful with the girls before, and this new found magnetism wasn't something he could easily toss away. There was a part of him that was quite adamant he didn't want to go back to being plain old Edward Gable.

"Edward!" Orson was out of his car, leaning against the driver's door. His big hands were casually stuffed in his jacket pockets. "How are you doing these days?"

"Fine. Have to go in," Edward muttered, eager to be alone.

"Haven't seen you in a while," Orson continued as Edward rudely walked straight by. "Got yourself a smart looking suit there. And you've got yourself a moustache. You've really been changing yourself."

Edward was at the door. He didn't want to talk to Orson at the moment.

"You remind me of someone else."

Edward stopped, his fingers on the handle. Orson made it sound like a threat. Slowly, he turned and walked across to the car. "What do you mean? Who do I remind you of?"

Orson looked up at him from under his eyebrows, but didn't answer. He had a cigarette balanced between his lips. Taking a lighter from his pocket, he lit up, shielding the naked flame with his hand. Inhaling, he took the cigarette away from his mouth and exhaled a fine twist of smoke. "Rita tells me you and your brother paid her a visit. Asking her about anonymous notes."

He should have known news would spread. That block of flats was so closely knit secrets would be difficult to keep. Besides which, Rita and Orson were constantly to be found within one another's flats. Orson was probably going to kick the crap out of him now for having threatened his woman.

Orson looked amused. "You're not in any trouble with me."

"Well, what do you want?" Edward asked huffily. "I already know who was sending those notes. The girl."

"The girl?"

"She lives across the landing from me."

Orson nodded knowingly. "So you haven't figured out who she is yet?"

Edward grew angry. Felt his fingers flex to fists.

Orson just smiled. "She didn't send you those notes."

"What? How would you know?"

He glanced up at the building, before flicking the cigarette to the ground and stubbing it out under the ball of his foot. He flicked his head down the road. "Walk with me."

They headed up the road away from the building and away from the residential area. Edward followed, a little hesitantly at first, then scurrying to keep up with Orson. This was the first time anyone had come to him, actually wanted to talk to him.

"So are you going to tell me who did send me those notes?"

"I did," Orson replied simply.

His answer threw Edward. Of all the people in the building, Orson struck him as the least afraid. Orson was big, domineering and confident in who he was.

"It was meant as a warning," Orson continued, ignoring Edward's look of shock. "A warning of things that may come if you hang around here long." He glanced over at Edward. "But I see things have already started."

"Are you threatening me? Are you saying I'm going to go the same way as Judy? Did someone kill her?"

Orson smiled bitterly. "Judy killed herself."

"So why ask who killed Kim Novak?"

"I wouldn't worry so much about Kim as about Judy Polwart. She threw herself in the river because she was depressed. She was fucked up to put it plainly. She was a quiet, impressionable girl when she moved in here. I don't think she felt she fitted in properly. She started changing the way she dressed, colouring her hair. Then she got her name changed. She didn't know who the hell she was supposed to be at the end of the day."

"And you think I'm going to top myself?"

"Oh, I never said you'll kill yourself. Different people deal with it in different ways. But you've changed the way you dress." He gave him an enquiring look. "Am I still talking to Edward?"

Edward ignored the screams of the letter in his rucksack. "I'm still legally Edward."

"Now there's an evasive answer if I ever heard one." Orson smiled to himself.

"It's all very well you being smug, but I don't see the point of all this secrecy, all these stupid letters. If you've got something to say, why not come out and say it?"

"Because I really didn't want to have to do it personally, but you just don't seem to have gotten the message."

"You? I don't see how you fit in. You don't come across like the suicidal type."

Orson snorted. "I'm not. But you don't seriously think I was born Orson Welles, do you?"

"Yeah, but someone like you wouldn't be pushed into changing his name."

"And how do you think the name Timo Jokinen would fit in a place like this?"

"Timo Joki..."

"It's Finnish," Orson explained.

"You're Finnish?" Edward breathed. "You wouldn't know to listen to you."

"What can I say? I am a master of languages," Orson shrugged off the compliment. "My name stuck out against all the English names when I came over here. Then I moved in this place, the Hollywood bloody walk of fame. I thought it would be a good laugh, you know? I'm an arts correspondence; do you see where I'm coming from? To be called Orson Welles, can you imagine the connection that comes with that? I thought it would be a cool thing to do."

"Did Sophia push you into it?"

"Sophia?" Orson laughed. "No one made me change my name. Now why would you pick on Sophia of all people?"

"She was the first one here, wasn't she?"

"No."

"So it's Archie?"

Orson laughed. "If you're looking for the beginning, I suppose you'd have to go to the landlady."

"The landlady? But I'm renting this from a property agent. Isn't everyone?"

"Ah, but it's still owned by someone, isn't it? I just think she likes to distance herself from it all. Madame Recluse, locked away up in the family home in Helmsley."

"She?"

"Miss Benson," Orson told him. "If you're wanting to go right back to the beginning, you want to start with Miss Benson."

"I'm just crazy about Tiffany's!"

So the girl had declared her allegiance whilst drinking cheap larger from a dented can. No one had been interested; it wasn't as if any of these young men would ever buy her diamonds. Her blonde hair had fallen loose of the plastic clips, but she was too drunk to care.

Edward watched her shuffle-dance by the television, his attention repetitively drifting to her posters, certain he had seen them before. Someone knocked a bowl of crisps onto the floor. Laughter, chatter, drinking, no one noticed. The girl started to trample the crisps into the carpet. Tomorrow morning, when she and her flatmate woke up hung over and crawled through into the living room, they'd realise the carpet was completely ruined and it would eventually come out of the deposit. Maybe Toby would be here; he looked as though he intended to sleep with one of the girls; but he wouldn't help clear up.

Edward felt sick. He'd drunk far too much. He didn't even know why he was here. He had been telling himself that he wanted to start putting some distance between himself and Toby. Between himself and the student life; university friends whom you just hung around with because you happened to share a flat or do the same course, friends six months after graduation you'd already forgotten all about.

Toby had caught him going home from work. Edward didn't make it home that evening. He'd been in a grim mood, a temperament ready for a lot of heavy drinking. He was still carrying the letters from deed poll about Clark Gable like an unborn child, his other self. He didn't dare rip the letter up, terrified the same thing would happen to him as had Marilyn, née Lexie.

He was Edward. Edward Gable. Or at least he thought he was. But the boy everyone associated with Edward was becoming a stranger to him. He didn't know who he was. Right now all he knew was he was drunk. Very drunk.

He drained his glass and stared up at the big black and white poster the girls had pinned up on their living room wall. It was the kind of thing you'd expect from girls like these: *Breakfast at Tiffany's* and Johny Depp. *Breakfast at Tiffany's*: he'd heard of it, heard of Audrey Hepburn, but had never seen the film and was only acquainted with it on a hearsay basis. The kind of thing that girls and femininely inclined men would be interested in.

Audrey Hepburn. Now, she was dead, he was sure of it. He gazed up at the image of the icon in his pickled state, knowing who it was, but at the same time sure he'd seen that look somewhere else before. Those big eyes. That image of classic innocence.

"Tequila!" Toby tripped onto the sofa, unsettling Edward and making his stomach lurch. Toby waved the half-drunk bottle like a toddler with a new toy. "We really, really need Tequila, right now. Hey," he added, poking Edward in the ribs with his elbow. "Do you remember Ant and his tequila?" He took a swig from the bottle. "What a wanker."

Edward took the bottle when offered, a clunk going down his throat and burning back up his windpipe.

"What's with the sideburns, anyway?" Toby asked. "You've gone weird the last few months. What is it with facial hair?"

"Never trust a man with a beard." The girl who liked Tiffany's had appeared in front of them, smiling provocatively at Toby.

Edward gave her an irritated look. He didn't know why he was here.

"At least you're not spending another weekend with those freaks," Toby laughed. "Dressed up like they're all off to black-tie 50s balls. What is all that about?"

"Oh, leave him alone," the girl said. "I think he's dressed really smartly. What's your name again?"

Edward looked up at her. He didn't know what to say. He didn't know. "I want to go home now," he told her before falling forward off the sofa and bumping his head on the floor.

The girl was giggling. Someone was saying that he'd had too much to drink. Who was that older guy anyway? Same age as everyone else? No, Debbie's only nineteen. Cold air rushed up in his face. Street lamps with greasy halos around them in the night. Diamonds are a girl's best friend. Film posters for *Breakfast at Tiffany's*. Audrey smiling at him with a long, slim cigarette holder at her lips. Audrey looked worried. What are you doing?

Edward belched loudly and wrinkled his nose at the smell that erupted from his mouth. He was lying on his back on what felt like cold hard concrete. He was inside somewhere, the electric light overhead. Holly Golightly was shaking him by the shoulders.

"Edward, are you all right? Can you hear me?"

He blinked and looked up at her, realising that he must be on the landing outside his flat. The girl was crouched down beside him, wrapped up in her silk dressing gown. She looked as though she'd just been woken up. Those big eyes gazed down at him in concern. They hadn't spoken since the argument and now she was here. He knew where he'd seen her before.

"I know who you are."

"Sorry?" She looked a little uncertain, her hands hovering near his shoulders. Ready to turn and run. He just gazed stupidly back at her.

"You need to get in your flat and lock the door. People do stupid things when they're drunk."

"I know who you are."

"Of course you do, we're neighbours."

Edward lurched up into her face as he sat up. "But who you've become."

She looked as though she was going to cry. "Edward…"

"I'm not Edward," he grumbled, lying back on the floor.

"What?"

"I'm Clark."

"What?" The girl leaned in closer, unable to clearly hear his drunken grumblings. "You're a clerk?"

"I'm Clark. Clark Gable."

Disappointment welled up in her eyes. She pushed herself away from him.

Edward closed his eyes and slipped away from consciousness, watching a line of Holly Golightlys knocking over bowls of diamonds and crushing them into the carpet.

Helmsley is a small market town out in the North Yorkshire Moors. Popular with pensioners on bus trips and bikers in the summer, it is a picturesque little sanctuary. With terrible bus connections.

Because of such appalling public transport services, Edward had been forced to take a ridiculously early bus that Saturday morning. He felt as though he had arrived before even the blackbirds had woken up. He had mooched around the small market square, peering in closed windows of secondhand and cut price bookshops, before going to sit on the steps of the stone market cross to wait for the business of the day to begin. He was going to find her, the woman Orson had suggested was at the root of all this madness.

He got directions from the tourist office; an afterthought squeezed in at the side of the entrance to Helmsley's ruined castle. With a hand-drawn map, he walked out into the residential edges of the town. The house was easy enough to find, even if it was tucked away from the road, surrounded by large privet hedges. There was a quiet, dignified air surrounding the property. Self-sufficient.

Edward was starting to feel nervous. He rang the doorbell and looked down at his shoes. This was to be the kind of introduction he had no idea how to begin. He'd dressed smartly for the day, in the first suit that Mr Chin had made for him. His hair was carefully combed, the moustache trimmed. But he looked tired, older than he was. He wasn't sleeping well these days.

The door opened. Edward looked up and from the first glance he knew he had come to the right place. A tall, slender woman in loose fitting clothes stood in the open doorway, calm and quiet. She had ivory skin, blue eyes and faultless blonde hair that waved down to run along her jaw line. A simple string of pearls around her neck. She was timelessly young.

"Miss Benson?"

She looked him up and down and smiled. "You must be Edward."

He hadn't rung ahead. "How do you know that?" In fact, this visit was so secretive, that she ought not to know he even had her address. James had got her details from the letting agency by some underhand means. He had barked his orders down the telephone line to Edward. Now that he'd got the address, something had to be done. He had to find out why he was living in the block of the deluded.

"Archie's told me all about you."

Archie. "You're still in touch with people at the flats?"

"Only Archie. He comes and visits quite regularly." She stepped back into the shadowy hallway. "Won't you come in?"

Miss Benson's house was cool inside, filled with refined antiquity that cried out quality, and above all else, old money. It was meditatively quiet as she lead him down the ticking corridor and out into the bright light of a walled garden. It felt so self-contained here as if the wider world had ceased to exist. She left him at a Victorian-looking set of wrought iron garden furniture and went back into the house.

Edward sat down and gazed up at the back of the imposing red brick building. Heavy drapes stood at either side of each darkened window. He could easily imagine that she lived alone here. A recluse.

Living off the profits of renting out property owned by the family.

Miss Benson soon returned carrying a tray with all the tea paraphernalia, and a cardboard shoe box that she offered no explanation for. She started to pour the tea. "Do you take sugar, Edward?"

"No, I…" He lent forward to take the tea cup, not sure how to begin, not even sure what he wanted to get from this meeting. "Miss Benson, don't you even want to know why I'm here?"

She smiled patiently and set the teapot down on the tray. "Let's dispense with the formalities. Miss Benson makes me sound like an old maid. Call me Grace."

Of course she would be Grace. James had made him look through a book of old film stars, to know the enemy, as James had put it. Edward thought that was a little harsh, but at least now he would be able to recognise people. Grace Kelly: Grace Benson.

"So you never changed your name all the way?"

Grace laughed lightly. "I've never changed my name at all. This is the name my mother gave me. She was fond of the name Grace. There was only myself and Archie there who had the names we were born with. Well, apart from Ray, but then he never fit the mould. Tell me, is he still called Ray?"

"Yes."

"It's reassuring to know he never changed it to Humphrey."

"So you're telling me Archie was born Archibald Leach and just happens to look like Cary Grant?"

She nodded. "It's just one of those coincidences. His mother happened to be very keen on Cary Grant, so I suppose there was a lot more purpose in that respect than with my name. Archie's a very genuine person. He was the first one outside the family to move into the building."

"So it was a family home?"

"Well, owned by the family. We never lived there as a family. My father bought the house as an investment. When my elder brother went to university, York University, my father had it converted into flats. My brother moved into the first flat finished for habitation, on the second floor. I started at the university two years later, and by then almost all of the flats were finished. I moved into the top floor. We thought about trying out leasing one of the flats, and Archie took it, the flat across from me."

"You lived in Sophia's flat?"

She nodded. "Archie used to come up to York regularly for business, so he'd decided a flat would be useful." Grace paused, smiling as she relived a memory she wouldn't share. "Over the next couple of years we got tenants for the other four flats. We had one of the ground floor flats as storage then." She opened the shoe box and took out a photograph, passing it to Edward. "There we all are. That was a few years ago now, of course."

Edward examined the photograph. It had been taken out doors, at a group picnic. It looked as though it had been taken in the Museum Gardens in the city centre. There was Grace, stood with a tall, blond man he presumed was her brother. Archie was instantly recognisable, just as he was now, with that charismatic smile. Ray was even in the picture, a little disgruntled as he always was. Three people were sitting on the park bench in the photo: a dumpy woman with lank blonde hair; an even larger woman with dark hair and bright eyes; and a bearded man with glasses and long hair tied back.

Apart from the three people he knew in the picture, no one looked like a film star. Edward put the photograph down. "So when did the obsession start?"

"The obsession?"

"Everyone looking like a film star."

"I suppose it was with Sophia, really," Grace started. "Although it never really began that way. She was lacking in confidence, wanted to make a few changes to her image, that was all. There was none of this making everyone in the building that way. I remember she had a lot of those coffee table books with her; you know the sort, with glossy photographs. Lots about old Hollywood. She soon latched on to the fact that I and Archie looked and were named what we were."

"But that's just coincidence, you say."

"Yes, it is. I suppose she just took some inspiration from that, and though she would get some fashion ideas from her books. It seemed perfectly harmless at the time. No one thought she would take it as far as it has gone."

"So this must have all started after you left."

"After I left?" Grace looked a little confused.

"Well, if you were living where Sophia is now…"

"Oh, Sophia moved into one of the first floor flats originally. She was our third tenant, you know. She was there before even Ray moved in."

"Ray…"

Grace pushed the photograph back across to him.

Edward looked down at the image.

"She's there in the picture."

Edward looked at the two women sat on the bench. Neither of them looked like Sophia.

"She lost quite a bit of weight after that photograph was taken."

"I realise she must have done, but even so, neither of these two look like Sophia."

"Sophia took the idea of changing herself all the way." Grace tapped at the image of the woman with the lank blonde hair. "She was called Abigail Simpson then."

"Abigail?" Edward couldn't believe the picture he was looking at had once been Sophia. "I realised she's English but, this…"

"You know she's English?" Grace looked surprised that he knew that much. "Archie tells me she's a very convincing Italian these days."

"I saw her passport in her flat."

"Ah," Grace nodded. "The only part she didn't manage to change. It all started out innocently enough, though. She got a new wardrobe, lost some weight and dyed her hair dark. She was very pretty; it would have been enough to leave it at that. But it wasn't Sophia-enough, at least she said so. She looked in the mirror and she still saw herself," Grace said sadly. "She started going to tanning salons to get that Italian skin. Started learning the language. There's nothing wrong with learning a language of course, but she didn't think she'd be the right kind of person until she spoke it fluently. She started affecting that accent when she spoke English. But it wasn't enough, and then she started spending money and Abigail just disappeared."

"You mean she got her name changed?"

"Well, yes, that and the plastic surgery."

Jesus. Edward looked down at the photograph. Sophia was nuts.

"Then she was finished, the image of her idol. But I suppose she still needed projects to do, or the daydream wasn't complete. Well, Archie was, but then she does idolise that man. Ray wouldn't have any of her nonsense of course. She started on me, telling me I should change my family name to Kelly. I can just imagine what Daddy would have had to say about that," Grace laughed uncomfortably. "Tom had moved out at that point. I didn't feel comfortable in my own home. Archie never really understood how serious Sophia's problem was. This little Chinese-Scottish woman moved in, and the way she dressed seemed to change overnight. Well, I just decided I had to get out, so I moved into our old family home. I didn't want to have to deal with the flats directly, so we passed all of that onto a letting agent."

"And Sophia moved up to your flat?"

"Oh yes," Grace said. For the first time negative human emotion showed on her face. Jealously. "She was crazy about Archie, still is from what I know. Wanted to be closer to him."

Edward felt deflated. "So why don't you just evict her? She's still at it, you realise? Lexie became Marilyn Monroe recently. This isn't healthy. You do realise someone topped themselves? Judy, or Kim Novak as she was known in her final days."

Grace lowered her eyes. "I know. She lived in your flat. But I don't think all the blame can be laid at Sophia's feet. In a way she's only trying to help people, give them confidence. Besides, the more people there who have changed, the harder it is for others to resist."

"But if Sophia wasn't there pestering people, this wouldn't be happening!" Edward was surprised by the strength of his own voice.

Grace went to pick up her teacup and saucer. The cup rattled in its dish. She put it back down again. "It's very hard to evict people."

"That's no excuse." He felt angry. Someone had to take responsibility and stop this. She was in the best position, owning the building. "You can't just let that mad house continue. One person's already killed themselves. Will someone else have to throw themselves into the river before you do anything?"

Grace looked genuinely upset, but with it was fear. There were probably a lot of reasons as to why she'd moved out. "Archie keeps an eye on it for me. We did worry just after Judy's body was found that Megan would soon follow, but Archie tells me she's settled down. You've been a good influence."

"Me?"

"Yes, on Megan." She paused. "You'll know her as Audrey."

The girl with the frightened eyes. "I don't actually know her as anything. *She's* never told me her name. I get the impression she's not actually capable of saying her name."

"I didn't realise that," Grace said quietly.

"So you're not going to do anything?"

"You're all right, though?" she responded, avoiding the question. "You're still Edward. Certainly there's a resemblance with Clark Gable, but…"

"I've had letters about my application to change my name to Clark."

"Oh. So you felt that you didn't fit in?"

"I never made the application. These letters have just turned up."

"Destroy them then; you'll be all right."

"The same thing happened to Lexie. She's now got a passport that says Marilyn Monroe."

Grace lent earnestly over the table. "Then move out. Get out of there before it's too late, before you forget who you really are."

"That's not really a solution to the long term problem. You need to deal with Sophia."

"There's nothing I can do about it." Grace avoided looking at his face. "You forget that the world isn't perfect. I can't fix all the problems."

"But…"

"No," she stopped him sharply. "Now please, I think we've come to the end of this." She held a hand up to her forehead, still refusing to look him in the eye. "I feel a migraine coming on. I think you should go."

Edward hung indecisively for a moment, furious that she wasn't prepared to take any responsibility. Then he stood up from the table. He would have to help himself.

"Goodbye, Grace."

He didn't have to wait long before the next bus departed for York. He got into the centre of town, and took a local bus home. He was filled with a new found maturity, like disillusionment in many ways, but certainly an inner peace.

He had hoped that he would be able to quietly slip into his flat without having to face anyone, but of course whenever your desperation is that high for good luck, fortune always hides somewhere, preferring instead to watch the chaos that can unfold.

Sophia was standing in the ground floor entrance. She was wearing shorts and a checked shirt, with a headscarf keeping her hair off her face. Stood akimbo over a plastic bag full of punnets of soft fruit, she was rooting through a shoulder bag for something.

She looked up as she saw the door open, her face brightening into a warm smile. With that look of sun-kissed innocence, Edward could have forgiven her almost anything. The moment wasn't to last.

"Hello there, Clark. How are you today?"

That little shred of vain hope that he was still overreacting disintegrated. "What?"

Sophia looked a little confused. "I asked you how you are."

"You called me Clark."

Her laugh tinkled merrily up the stairwell. "No I didn't. You must be hearing things, Edward." Pulling her keys from her bag, she leaned forward and picked up her bag full of raspberries. "Wouldn't it be funny if you were called Clark, though? Then you'd be Clark Gable." She faltered, uncertain about the expression on Edward's face. He'd never looked this forceful, this sure of himself before. She moved for the stairs.

"Like Sophia Loren?" he asked as she turned her back on him.

"Sorry?" It was clear she didn't want to have this conversation. She started up the staircase.

Edward's voice was flat and steady. "It would be funny if I were called Clark Gable in the way you're called Sophia Loren."

"People can find the strangest things funny." She kept on walking.

Edward stepped up to the foot of the stairs. He was angry. Like a child with a tantrum, he wanted to be cruel. Whether she really deserved it or not was debatable. "See you around then, Abigail."

Sophia stopped at the turn of the staircase, her hand hovering just above the railing. "What did you say?"

"See you around then."

Nodding to herself, convincing herself that all was well, she started to move again.

"Abigail Simpson."

Sophia swung around, her eyes like vipers. A snap change in personality. "Who have you been talking to?" she demanded, her put-on Italian accent making haughty work of the vowels. Even though she knew he knew, she couldn't drop the act. Maybe she'd forgotten how to.

"I went to visit our landlady today. Grace Benson."

"That whore?" Sophia shrieked. Red fury was flickering under her tan. "That conniving little tramp? I suppose she told you he really loves her; that he just spends time with me because he feels sorry for me."

"I don't know about that. But I did find out about Abigail Simpson and this charade you've put the whole building under."

"I don't make anyone do anything!" Sophia shouted, shrinking back as Edward made a move to come up the staircase. "How dare you go snooping into my past like that." Her hands started to ball up into fists.

"Considering people have been driven to self-destruction, I don't think…"

"Shut up!" Sophia howled. Consumed by fury, she drove a hand into her bag, raspberry juice draining down between her fingers as she clenched her fist. She flung the slop at Edward as he put a foot on the first step. "You keep away from me!" she shrieked. "You consort with half-brained tarts, then this is what you get!"

Edward lowered his eyes, watching the crushed raspberries slide down the front of his suit, leaving a stained pink trail, before slopping and dropping to the floor, limp and inert. He looked back up at Sophia. Steel gaze.

A mixture of anger and terror met his look. "That's no more than you deserve, you beast." Sophia threw before charging up the stairs before he had chance to even consider pursuit.

Edward looked back down at his suit. He probably deserved it in a way. Sophia was completely messed up. Even so, he still couldn't believe that she'd honestly meant any of it maliciously. But he wouldn't be able to stay here anymore. He really would have to move out.

Trudging up to the first floor, he paused outside his flat and gazed around the landing. Thinking over the last few months, the people he had met here and the things they had done. The things they had said and argued over. He looked over at the girl's door. He had two names for her now: Audrey and Megan, but he still didn't know what to call her. Not that she was speaking to him anymore.

The latch twisted and the door opened. The girl stepped out onto the landing. She had a folded newspaper in one hand, her handbag in the other. She looked at him shyly. "Edward," she started. "I heard shouting."

"Yeah," he sighed, flicking the remains of the final raspberry that was still clinging on. "It was Sophia. We had to clear the air about a couple of things." He paused, feeling awkward. It had been a few weeks since they had properly spoken. "I'm sorry. I know it's a bit late now, but I shouldn't have said…"

"No." She held up a hand, shaking her head. "You were probably right. It gave me a lot to think about." She stuck the newspaper up like a baton. "I've even been looking for flats. I'm going to move out. Be myself again."

"Megan?"

Her face broke out into a wide, captivating smile.

Edward stuck his hands in his jacket pocket. Feeling a little too self-aware. "I should probably start looking for somewhere new to live as well. I can't stay here. This place seems to make a habit of driving people mad."

"You could come flat hunting with me."

"I could."

"I was going to go look at a couple in Haxby."

"I could go have a look at what else there is to offer in the vicinity." Edward nodded to himself. "We could look for new places to live together."

"Move out together."

It hadn't really been conscious, but they'd been taking steps across the landing as they'd agreed with each other's suggestions. They were now stood directly in front of one another.

"Today can be the start of the rest of our lives."

"We need to get out of here before we completely loose our minds." He felt alive again, hopeful. Young and expectant of all the things he could do. He forgot himself, grabbing her hands. "We should run away. Right now."

"Right now?"

"Right now. Together."

"You can't do that."

They looked up to see an angry Sophia leaning forward over the banister, far above them. She hadn't gone back into her flat, but had hidden, listening and worrying about what was going to happen.

The girl gazed up and looked Sophia in the eye for the first time in a long while. "I think you'll find we will."

"But you can't!" Sophia howled in agony. "Clark Gable and Audrey Hepburn were never in a film together."

"And we really couldn't give a damn what they didn't do."

With grins on their faces, and a whoop from the girl, they ran down the staircase, almost too fast, almost stumbling and tripping to the ground, only just managing to keep their balance. Bursting through the doors, they rushed out into the fresh air, running hand in hand down the street. The wind blew through her hair. Crossing over the road, they left the tarmac and ran onto the grass of a small green area. Coming to a halt, gazing up at the sky. The light was intense, powerful like just after a storm; the trees lit up against a backdrop of violently painted clouds.

The girl looked over at the boy and smiled. "So what happens now?"

www.ingramcontent.com/pod-product-compliance
Lightning Source LLC
Chambersburg PA
CBHW050819180626
46814CB00004B/1364